BO

DOES BARNABAS HAVE THE POWER TO SAVE MAGGIE'S LIEE?

Dr. Giles Collins must have Maggie Evans's blood if he is to proceed with his mysterious experiments— experiments which have thus far resulted in many, many deaths.

Maggie, fearing for her life, turns to Barnabas Collins for help although she has been warned that he is a vampire and may also be after her life's blood.

But though Maggie's fate rests in his hands, Barnabas can do little for her, because his life is also endangered by Giles Collins!

Hermes Press

Published by Hermes Press, an imprint of
Herman and Geer Communications, Inc.

Daniel Herman, Publisher
Troy Musguire, Production Manager
Eileen Sabrina Herman, Managing Editor
Alissa Fisher, Graphic Design
Kandice Hartner, Senior Editor

2100 Wilmington Road
Neshannock, Pennsylvania 16105
(724) 652-0511
www.HermesPress.com; info@hermespress.com

Book design by Eileen Sabrina Herman
First printing, 2020

LCCN applied for: 10 9 8 7 6 5 4 3 2 1 0
ISBN 978-1-61345-217-2
OCR and text editing by H + G Media and Eileen Sabrina Herman
Proof reading by Eileen Sabrina Herman and Gavin Scott

From Dan, Louise, Sabrina, Jacob, Ruk'us and Noodle for D'zur and Mellow

*Acknowledgments: This book would not be possible without the help and
encouragement of Jim Pierson and Curtis Holdings*

Printed in Canada

THE PHANTOM AND BARNABAS COLLINS
by Marilyn Ross

CONTENTS

CHAPTER 1

They had entered the tomb as the evening shadows were deepening. Slim, dark-haired Maggie Evans looked awed as she breathed the dank air of the dark underground burial place and peered into the gloom to make out the strange surroundings. At her side, erect and handsome in a black caped coat, Barnabas Collins held a flickering candle aloft.

In his resonant voice with its suggestion of a British accent, he told her, "This place has great meaning for me."

"You say this is the tomb of Dr. Giles Collins?" she asked.

Barnabas nodded gravely. "Yes, Maggie, I came across him in one of the family histories. He lived here at Collinwood almost a century ago."

"I have never heard his name mentioned."

He smiled slightly. "Nor that of Valeria Norris, either, I wager."

"That name is also strange to me." Maggie stared at his strong profile in the flickering glow of the candle. Since his arrival from England to be a guest at Collinwood, she had been fascinated by this charming distant cousin of Elizabeth's. And he had seemed to take a liking to her.

Even when she'd first met Barnabas, he seemed to know all about her and her problems.

Indeed, he seemed to understand all the people in the great forty-room mansion that dominated the cliffs overlooking the sea. From the moment he and his elderly manservant had taken up residence in the somber smaller house situated between Collinwood and the private family cemetery, he'd come to have a strange influence on each of them.

There were times when she suspected him of being both a hypnotist and a mind reader. His strange, penetrating eyes would fasten on her and she seemed to be completely captivated by him. She knew the residents of the small Maine fishing town whispered about him behind his back. Rarely, if ever, did he leave the old house during the daylight hours, but once dusk came he would take solitary walks about the grounds of the great estate.

Often he would call in at Collinwood itself and spend an hour or two in discussion with Elizabeth Stoddard or Roger Collins. Frequently Maggie would find herself drawn into these conversations, which she invariably enjoyed. Carolyn considered Barnabas "a truly groovy character," so perhaps the lad, David, Maggie's charge, was the only one in the mansion not impressed by him. David was too occupied with his young boy's interests and enthusiasms to notice much else.

Only that afternoon Maggie had gone for a picnic with Carolyn and David, at an isolated section of beach not far from Widow's Hill. And while David had kept himself busy trying to get a homemade kite to fly properly, Maggie and Carolyn had sat on blankets in their bathing suits and talked.

It was early August and warm and sunny. Raising herself on an elbow, Carolyn said, "Barnabas has been telling me about London. I wish Mother would let me go to college there."

Maggie smiled at her. "London is a great distance away."

"I know," Carolyn said. "But surely Cousin Barnabas will be returning there. And he could keep an eye on me and show me around."

"I don't know. His plans seem very vague. He hasn't spoken of returning to England. He seems to have traveled a great deal."

"He's been everywhere," Carolyn said with girlish enthusiasm. "I think he's the most fascinating man I've ever met."

Maggie stared out at the ocean and a lone small sailing ship with red and white sails veering towards the Collinsport harbor. "I know how you feel," she said. "There's a quality of mystery about him which gives him appeal."

"I'm sure Mother and Uncle Roger are impressed by him as well," the green-eyed Carolyn said, clasping her hands around her bent, tanned knees. "Of course they won't admit it. Especially Uncle Roger! He's so determined to be the important one of the family."

Maggie laughed. "You're becoming quite a judge of character."

"Not really," Carolyn said. "Uncle Roger is pretty obvious, that's all."

"I enjoy talking to Barnabas," Maggie admitted.

"Of course you do," Carolyn said. "I've seen you two together. You hang on his every word."

"He knows so much about Collinwood. About its history and those who lived here in the past."

Carolyn sighed. "He even resembles that painting of his ancestor in the main hallway. He was pleased when I told him that."

They probably would have continued their discussion if David hadn't come back. His kite experiment wasn't working out and he enlisted Maggie's aid to see if together they might get it to fly. Eventually they did, but by that time the late afternoon air had been chilled by the approach of fog. A white cloud on the horizon, at the start, the rolling mist swept toward the beach, cutting off the overhead sun and making it cold. They had quickly gathered up their things and made their way to the house with the distant foghorn providing a melancholy background sound.

By dinner time the fog had settled thickly. The striking view from Collinwood was shut off by a weird curtain of mist and the great shade trees dripped with moisture.

For some reason Maggie was caught up by a feeling of restlessness after the evening meal, and taking her rain cloak, embarked on a solitary stroll.

Once outside, she almost decided to give up the idea. The fog was thicker than she'd anticipated; there was almost a drizzle coming down. And it would soon be dark. But she felt the urge to get out of the house and talk to someone. Perhaps Barnabas might be out for his evening walk, she decided. And the prospect of meeting him made up her mind. She lifted the hood of the cloak over her hair and went on down the steps.

Since her best hope of meeting him would be on the path between Collinwood and the old house where he lived with his single manservant, she walked that way, past the several outbuildings and along the narrow path to the ancient dark house. When she came abreast of it she paused to stare at its somber outline wreathed in the vapory fog. The windows were shuttered and showed no light, giving her the feeling they were heavy-lidded malevolent eyes. The door was closed and grimly austere.

She debated whether to knock. Then the sound of a soft footstep in the shadows behind her made her wheel about. It was Barnabas. Moisture gleamed on his dark hair and on the silver head of the cane he carried.

"I thought I would be the only one mad enough to be abroad on such an evening," he said, smiling.

"There's an eerie attraction about a night like this," she confessed. "Besides, I hoped that we would meet."

"I'm glad we have," he said. "I was in a somber mood. You will be good for me."

"Elizabeth has warned me not to stray far from the house," Maggie explained. "You've heard about the several attacks made on young women during the past few weeks."

"Yes," he said, "I have heard about them. And I can understand why she would be worried."

Maggie smiled apologetically. "I don't feel nervous. And nothing really awful happened to those other girls. I think their stories may be made up. They all run along the same lines. One of them may have hit on the idea for attention and the others repeated her account."

"Possibly," Barnabas said, studying her.

She felt uneasy under his solemn stare. "I mean, it is a pretty wild story—a mysterious man appearing in the darkness to seize them and bite them on the throats. And their accounts are so confused and dazed as to the facts. I think it has to be some sort of hoax. But Elizabeth is taking it quite seriously."

"You might be wise to heed her. There are many strangers in the village at this time of year."

"Perhaps you're right." Her tone was doubtful.

He smiled. "At any rate, you needn't worry now that I have joined you. I was about to walk as far as the family cemetery. Does that suggestion repel you on this inclement night?"

Maggie did not mind where they went so long as she would have his company and conversation. So she said, "Not at all. I know you visit there often."

"It has a special interest for me," he told her with a thoughtful expression on his handsome, sallow face. "As you know, I'm spending all my days compiling a history of the Collins family."

"Elizabeth mentioned that," she acknowledged as they began to stroll along side by side. "Roger considers you're wasting your time."

"Indeed," Barnabas commented wryly. "Well, Roger is not a very sensitive or understanding fellow. So I'll not worry about him."

"I'm sure I wouldn't. Only it seems to me you're working too hard at it. You never see the sunlight. And we are having some lovely days this summer."

"Believe me, I miss them," he assured her. "But I have no time to waste. I must press on with my work so that it is finished before I leave."

"I hope that won't be too soon," she said. "You've made it so much more interesting for us here. Carolyn was saying only this afternoon she'd like to go to college in London to be near you when you returned there."

He smiled. "That is indeed a tribute. But I may not return to London directly when I leave here."

"I warned her of that."

"Did you?" He looked at her with interest as they walked on. "You know, it is you whom I feel to be closest to me. You have my liking for the quiet and solitude. I noticed it soon after I came here."

She was flattered; she had the same feeling of comradeship for him.

They passed the rise in the broad field and started down the slope to the iron-fenced family cemetery with the woods beyond it. In the fog she had difficulty making out the clutter of tombstones and monuments that marked the graves of long dead members of the family. Far away the foghorn droned its melancholy warning. All in all, it was a good night for ghosts to emerge from the moss-covered mounds and make their shadowy ways among the tilted and weathered headstones.

Abruptly she asked Barnabas, "Do you believe in ghosts?"

He paused and frowned slightly. "I believe there is another life, one we do not fully understand as yet. And that the denizens of that unknown world have a decided influence on us."

"Of course you would think that. You are so linked to the past."

"I am," he said with great emphasis. "Even more so than you might believe."

She smiled wryly. "When I was a child one of the older girls tried to scare me with tales of phantoms and bony hands reaching out of the darkness to grip me. I suppose it made a lasting impression on my young mind."

Barnabas nodded. "And yet you do not strike me as one with a fear of the unknown."

"I'm caught somewhere between fear and fascination," she confessed. "I have often come to the cemetery here alone. And when I read the old gravestones I almost was able to picture the people they described and feel their sadness."

The deep-set eyes bored into her. "Interesting." Then they walked on.

As they entered the open gate of the old graveyard a chilling touch of fear swept through her. Somehow the influence of the dead, which Barnabas had referred to, seemed to fill the damp, shadowed night. Barnabas strode forward between the closely set graves with their various stones and she followed.

He walked so quickly and with such purpose she had difficulty in keeping up with him. At last he paused before a large gray tomb in a remote corner of the cemetery she had never ventured to before. The tomb was almost concealed with vines, glistening now from the damp fog.

"This is the Giles Collins tomb," he said. "I'm dealing with him in my book now. So I'm particularly interested in it at the moment."

Studying the worn lettering on the front of the tomb she was barely able to make out the name. "I have never noticed it before."

"Then you have missed something," he said. "I have explored the tomb many times for details to put in my book. You may be interested to know that it has a hidden chamber."

She looked at him. "A hidden chamber?"

"Yes. There is a story associated with it, of course. But why don't I show it to you?"

All at once she had an unexplainable desire to shrink back and refuse to go any further. The panic that had been welling up in her since she'd entered the confines of the fog-shrouded cemetery became almost uncontrollable. Her heart began to pound strangely. "I'm not sure that I want to go in there."

But his hand was on her arm, holding it gently yet firmly. "I think you should," he said in a persuasive tone.

He reached out to lift the rusted latch of the ancient iron door guarding the tomb. It was not locked; the door opened with a creaking protest to reveal the complete blackness of the tomb entrance.

"There are a few steps to descend," he said in the same calm voice as he guided her carefully down the uneven, moss-covered stone steps.

She still wanted to hold back but somehow she was no longer in control of her actions. Barnabas Collins had robbed her of her will. She was mutely obeying him now, behaving like a puppet.

When they reached the bottom of the steps to stand in the lower level of the tomb she was aware of the dank odor of decay in the air. It was a frightening place and she couldn't see anything.

Barnabas said, "I'll light a candle. I keep some here for the purpose of my explorations."

He released her arm as he went about finding the candle and lighting it. But she was much too terrified to make a move. He held the candle aloft so that she could see the neat rows of coffins on either side, resting on shelves reaching to the ceiling of the tomb. Now in a low tone Barnabas explained these were the caskets containing the remains of Dr. Giles Collins and his immediate family.

"I did not know there had been a doctor among the Collins ancestors."

"Indeed there was," Barnabas said, his handsome face strangely lighted by the flickering glow of the candle. "And next you shall see the hidden chamber."

Again he took her by the arm and propelled her forward. They reached what appeared to be a solid stone wall, but when he touched one of the stones an opening was soundlessly revealed—a doorway hardly as high as her head.

"You must crouch to go through," Barnabas said as he gently pushed her into the unknown darkness once more.

She wanted to scream, but didn't wish to appear childish or craven in his eyes. He bent low to follow her through the secret entrance and they were standing together in a smaller tomb with a single shelf and a lone casket on it.

"This is the coffin of the Valeria Norris I mentioned," he told her. "It is worth examining more closely."

"But why is she buried here? In this hidden tomb?" Maggie inquired with a slight tremor in her voice.

Barnabas smiled grimly. "I'll tell you about that later. Come." And he led her across the murky room to the casket.

The coffin rested on a shelf about two feet above the stone floor of the tomb. It was covered with dust and cobwebs stretched from its ends and sides to join with the walls. As Maggie came close a cobweb from above touched her cheek like a ghostly finger. She gave a start and cried out.

Barnabas laughed lightly. "You must not be so nervous. I have come to look upon spiders and their webs as friendly things."

"I didn't see it," Maggie told him weakly.

They were standing by the casket now and Barnabas was regarding it with almost a reverent expression. "You will notice that it is unusually fine. The wood is richly polished beneath the dust. And though the nameplate is tarnished, it is exquisitely designed."

She saw that the dust had been removed from the nameplate and she could make out the scroll lettering. "Valeria Norris."

Looking up into the gaunt face of the man beside her, she asked, "Who was she?"

"A beauty like yourself who lived at Collinwood long ago. She played an important role in its history."

"And she was buried in a secret tomb?"

"Yes."

"For some special reason?" Maggie persisted. "Why should she have been buried away from the others?"

Barnabas gave her a mocking glance. "I was certain you

would be anxious to hear her story."

"You make it sound as if there was some mystery connected with her death and her being buried alone in this place."

"I believe Asa Collins arranged it because he felt it would have been the wish of Dr. Giles Collins, his son. He could not bring himself to have Valeria buried in the main body of the family tomb, but in this chamber set aside he was able to accept the idea."

Maggie's eyes were wide with wonder. Momentarily she had forgotten the weird surroundings and her fears. All her attention was drawn to this part of Collinwood's history of which she'd had no previous knowledge.

"Then Asa Collins must have disliked this Valeria."

"He did," Barnabas agreed. "He blamed her for the death of his son. And though there was a continual friction between the old ship owner and his doctor son, the old man was very fond of Giles. His sudden death must have been a terrible blow to him."

Maggie glanced toward the ancient coffin with its dust and cobwebs again. "Did she kill Giles?"

Wax was dripping down from the burning candle and a trickle of it touched the clay-colored hand holding it, but Barnabas appeared not to notice this. He fixed his eyes on Maggie's in that odd, hypnotic manner of his. The burning eyes under the bushy dark brows held her full attention; she was unable to move or speak. She stood there staring at him in dazed fascination.

He went on talking in his low, rich voice, but his words blurred together and she made no sense of them. The brilliant, penetrating eyes made her feel slightly dizzy. Reality slipped away from her. Gradually the level of his voice seemed to increase; his warm tones embraced her and there was a sound like rushing water clamoring in her ears. She raised a hand to press against her temple. Her fingers seemed numbed and as she took her hand away it somehow floated in the shadowed darkness. And after that it was all darkness and she was in the midst of it.

A querulous elderly female voice penetrated the black velvet saying, "I'm sure she stirred just now."

"Yes, she's coming around," a younger masculine voice replied in a strained fashion.

Maggie opened her eyes, not knowing just what had happened or where she was. Her mind was filled with confusion. Somewhere an eternity ago a handsome, dark man with piercing eyes had been standing gazing at her. Those eyes remained vivid in her memory although all the other details seemed to have vanished. The eyes had fixed on hers and all else had become blurred.

She stared up with alarm at the man bending over her. The eyes that gazed at her gravely now were not those that still haunted her. These eyes were blue and concerned and the face of the man was that of a stranger. A blond, good-looking male in his early thirties with fine, sensitive features.

In a weak voice she asked him, "Who are you?"

His face brightened. "Excellent! So you are able to talk."

Her eyes wandered from him to the stout, elderly woman standing anxiously a few feet behind him. She wore a neat lace cap on her drawn-back white hair. Maggie's eyes widened as she realized that the elderly woman was wearing a quaint, voluminous brown dress which reminded her of illustrations from some ancient book.

And this made her shift her glance to the man bending over her and recognize that his neat gray suit was in the fashion of an era unfamiliar to her.

Maggie raised herself on an elbow and stared about the room. At once she recognized it as the rear parlor of Collinwood. Some of the articles of furniture such as the sideboard and the chaise longue across from her were familiar. And the portraits of the early members of the family hung in their proper places on the wall. Yet there was something oddly changed in the room.

Her eyes wandered to the table in the room's center and she saw that a lamp shaded with a large yellow globe provided the main source of soft light. And the wallpaper was different and so was the rug. She couldn't understand it.

"What happened?" she asked the young man.

"Don't you remember?" He was studying her closely.

She touched the back of her hand to her forehead, partially covering her eyes as she strained to recall something of the past. "No," she confessed. "My mind seems to be a blank."

The elderly woman came forward a step. "I don't like this, Giles. I'm sure she must be badly injured."

"Now we mustn't allow our nerves to get the better of us. Aunt Polly," he remonstrated.

"But the girl is confused and obviously hurt."

"We'll find that out." He turned to Maggie once more. She saw that he wore a broad, crimson tie and a high collar. He asked her, "Are you sure you can't remember anything?"

"Nothing," she assured him, "beyond the fact that this is Collinwood and my name is Maggie Evans."

The two exchanged a glance. Then the blond man addressed her again. "You've recalled your name. Try to remember what happened."

"But I can't!" she said desperately.

"Think hard," he said.

"I tell you I'm completely bewildered! My mind is in a

whirl!" she said with spirit. She indicated the room with a wave of her hand. "And what have you done to this room? It seems so very much different."

The old woman came forward to gaze at her grimly. "I insist that this girl's mind has been injured in the accident!" she said. "Not a thing has been done to this room since she went out riding with Valeria this afternoon."

The blond man nodded at Maggie. "I'm afraid that's true."

She sat up now, sure that they were both mad. "What is this talk about my going riding? And who is Valeria?"

The old woman gave a sharp cackle of laughter. "That settles it. If she doesn't recognize the name of her best friend there has to be something wrong with her."

The man gave the stout woman a reproving look. "I wish you'd let me handle this. After all, I am a doctor."

"And not showing much indication of it at this moment," the old woman replied in a vinegar tone.

Ignoring her, the man sat down on the divan next to Maggie and took her hand in his. "Tell me my name."

She looked at him blankly. "I don't know."

"Come now! Try hard!" he urged. "Perhaps then all the rest will fall into proper place."

"I have tried," she said in a voice near tears.

"Please."

Maggie bowed her head. "I don't know who you are," she said. "Or what I'm doing here."

There was a slight pause. Then he said gently, "My name is Giles Collins. Dr. Giles Collins. And you are here as the guest 'of my sister-in-law, Valeria Norris."

"Valeria Norris!" she exclaimed. "Yes, that name has a familiar ring." She hesitated. "But somehow I feel it belongs to a girl who died long ago."

The young doctor smiled sadly. "You're still confused, Maggie. Valeria is very much alive in this year 1880."

CHAPTER 2

"1880," Maggie echoed in a tone of disbelief. The year did not seem right to her.

Giles Collins nodded. "August the third, to be exact," he said.

She struggled with this for a moment. Everything seemed different and strange. Yet here were these people in familiar surroundings calling her by her name and seemingly well-informed about her background. Could it be that she'd had an accident severe enough to blot out important details from her mind?

For the first time she gave attention to her own dress. Long-skirted and flowing, it was a green riding habit with a white jabot.

She looked up at the blond man. She said, "It seems I have lost my memory. What sort of accident did I have?"

"You were riding Raven," he said. "You and Valeria were crossing the field from Widows' Hill when the stallion took fright at something and galloped out of control. According to Valeria, you tumbled from the saddle almost at once."

Aunt Polly showed a disapproving expression on her wrinkled face with its mottled brown spots. "I warned you, Giles. That black devil is no proper mount for the girl. But you wouldn't listen!"

Giles Collins turned to the old woman with a pained expression on his sensitive features. "I have heard that enough, Aunt Polly. Would you be so good as to go get a pot of strong, hot tea for Maggie?"

The old woman hunched her shoulders indignantly. "I know it's your way of getting rid of me. But I'll do as you say." With her lips set in a firm line she marched out of the room.

Giles turned to Maggie and spread his hands. "She is a difficult old woman. But as my father's only remaining sister she has a place in the house. I hope you don't find her too tedious!"

She managed a wan smile. "Not at all," she said. "I feel very stupid not remembering anything this way."

"As a medical man I can promise you this is a fairly common result of an accident of the type you suffered. You should not be alarmed. Your general condition seems good and your color is returning. Does your head ache from the actual bump?"

She touched a hand to the region where her head throbbed. "There is a lump there," she admitted. "It's tender, but my head doesn't ache."

"Excellent. I checked while you were still unconscious and found there were no abrasions."

Maggie blushed slightly. "I'm sorry to be such a nuisance."

"Not at all," he said with a frown. "Aunt Polly was right in at least one thing. It was stupid of me to send you out on Raven. In the future you'll be given one of the mares. We have two young and gentle ones."

"You mentioned Valeria," she said. "I'm afraid I can't remember her either. Where is she?"

"She was very shocked by your accident," the young doctor told her. "So I gave her a sleeping draught and sent her up to her room to rest for the night. And that would appear to be the wisest treatment for you as well."

"You forget that you sent your aunt to fetch me tea," she reminded him with a twinkle in her dark eyes.

He smiled. "Aunt Polly won't be surprised to arrive and find you gone. She suspected my motives in any case. Let me assist you up to your room and give you something to make you sleep until the morning."

Maggie rose and stood uneasily until he gave her his arm for support. She was still more lightheaded than she'd realized.

The bedroom to which the young man escorted her was on the third floor of the great mansion. It was furnished in elegant good taste with a large four poster bed and canopy. A huge white marble fireplace graced the wall opposite the bed and two windows overlooked the cliffs and the ocean. An ornate oil lamp on a bedside table provided the small area of soft light in the large shadowed room. She saw that a maid had neatly turned the bed down.

She stood for a moment taking it all in and then told Dr. Giles Collins, "It's as if I've never been in here before."

"I can promise you that you have. You've occupied this same room ever since you came here from Boston a month ago."

Maggie felt awkward. "I'm sure I'll remember everything in the morning."

"I hope so," he agreed. "It could take longer. Just don't let it worry you."

"I'll try not to," she told him. "It's a stupid question, I'm sure, but just why did I come here?"

"You're the guest of my sister-in-law, Valeria. She brought you with her when she returned from Boston. She has been living with me since the death of my wife."

"Forgive my bringing up any painful memories," she murmured.

His sensitive face had shadowed. "Losing Olive was a shattering business. But Valeria is much like her. And having her here is helping me. They were very close, even for sisters."

"I shall look forward to talking with Valeria in the morning."

Giles smiled. "That sounds so strange—you two are always having your private chats. By morning you may have come back to your normal state. Just now I'll mix you that sleeping potion."

Going to the dresser, he took a small bottle of white liquid from the neat medical bag he'd brought upstairs with him. He mixed the liquid with some water from a pitcher left on the dresser and then came over to her with it.

She took it gingerly. "Are you certain I require this?"

"I think it will help you recover from the shock and hasten the return of your memory."

Obediently she drained the contents of the glass. The liquid had an odd almond flavor.

The young doctor took the empty glass from her. "By the time you're ready for bed the potion should be taking effect."

"Thank you," she said. "Forgive my stupidity and the trouble I've caused you all."

"No trouble," he protested. "And you shouldn't apologize. It's really my fault for letting you ride the stallion. Sleep well." He bowed and went out leaving her alone in the dimly lighted room.

It was the first moment she'd been by herself since regaining consciousness. She earnestly hoped that morning would bring her full recollection. Frightened and desperately weary, she quickly began to prepare for bed.

By the time her head touched the pillow the potion was starting to work. Her vision was fuzzy and she was surrendering to an engulfing tide of drowsiness. All her worry and concerns faded as she sank into a deep, satisfying slumber.

But it was not to be a sleep bereft of dreams. As the hours passed she stirred restlessly in the darkness of the canopied bed. Nightmares took her to another Collinwood —a Collinwood dominated by the matronly beauty, Elizabeth Stoddard, and where the handsome dark stranger, Barnabas Collins, was a guest.

She dreamed of walking with Barnabas Collins through a fog-laden night, of arriving at a remote tomb and reading the name "Valeria Norris" on the plate of a dust-laden coffin. And then she was overwhelmed by a feeling of being suffocated and begged Barnabas Collins to let her leave the tomb. But the handsome dark man stood blocking her way. She screamed and tried to push past him!

She wakened to find herself sitting up in bed. It took her a moment to remember that only a few hours ago the kindly young doctor had brought her to this room. It was still night and dark— so dark she could barely make out the marble fireplace set in the opposite wall.

As she peered into the blackness she suddenly had a feeling of apprehension. Of not being alone! A cold clamminess had crept into the room with the shades of night. Fearfully she let her eyes roam until she saw the shadow to the right of her bed. Her fingers clutched the edge of the sheets as the shadow seemed to hover and then advance slowly towards her. Her eyes adjusting to the darkness, she was able to make out the eerie figure stepping slowly up to her bedside. A figure clothed in pink!

As the pink phantom moved closer to her, she saw its loose flowing robe and cowl that shielded but did not completely conceal the wizened hag's face. Its look of hatred wrenched a scream from Maggie's lips.

At the sound of the scream the apparition hurriedly stepped back, vanishing into the shadows. Chilled by the horror of what she'd seen, not certain whether she'd been visited by a ghost or by a figment of her imagination, Maggie sat staring into the dark. The thing had disappeared as quickly as it had shown itself. Would she put it down to a product of her confused mental state and the sleeping potion?

It was hard to make up her mind. Aware that she was trembling, Maggie forced herself to sink back on the pillow. Even then sleep did not come to her until her eyelids drooped from sheer exhaustion.

The second time she awakened it was morning and someone was knocking on the door. Sitting up in bed, she invited her caller in. At once the door opened and Aunt Polly entered, accompanied by a nervous-looking maid of youthful appearance carrying a large breakfast tray.

"Put it on the bed," the old woman ordered the girl.

The maid obeyed with an uneasy smile for Maggie as she removed the silver coverings from its steaming plates. The breakfast was huge by Maggie's standards. As soon as the maid went out she told Aunt Polly so.

The stout old woman shrugged. "Eat what you can, then. Are you feeling any better?"

"Yes, I am," Maggie said. "But my memory still seems blacked out."

Aunt Polly regarded her with sharp eyes. "It's my opinion you should have extra medical care. But I can't convince my stubborn nephew Giles of that. So it seems you must suffer your illness through. When you need the maid, ring the bell rope by the head of your bed. It's to the left."

"Thank you," Maggie told the old woman's retreating back. She saw that there indeed was a bell rope but doubted that she'd have any use for it.

She enjoyed the hot porridge and ate as much as she could of the hearty breakfast, still preoccupied with the eerie visitation during the night. It was so vivid to her that she began to doubt that it had been a nightmare. But then, nightmares could be frighteningly real and this one had surely seemed to possess that quality.

This whole existence in which she found herself had the uncanny quality of a dream. She felt she'd been transplanted into a different world in which everyone knew all about her but in which she remained a stranger. The young doctor had promised her this mental fuzziness would soon pass and in the meantime she would have to manage as best she could. But it was embarrassing.

She had finished breakfast, washed and put on a crisp orange dress when the second knock came on her door. This time she opened it herself to find a strikingly pretty black-haired girl smiling at her from the hallway.

"How are you feeling, Maggie?" the girl in white asked, coming into the room. Her hair had a touch of curl and was gathered at the nape of her neck with a white ribbon.

Maggie smiled forlornly. "I feel well enough. But the accident has left me without any memory at all."

"Oh, no!" the girl protested, looking shocked.

"I'm afraid so. For instance, you could be any pretty stranger rather than my good friend, Valeria Norris. Luckily, Giles says it will pass, that in due time I will be able to remember."

"I was almost hysterical with fear when you tumbled from your saddle."

"So Giles said."

Valeria looked anxious. "Perhaps you should have remained in bed."

"No, I don't think so," she said. "I'm sure getting outside will do me good."

"I hope you're right. It is a lovely, sunny morning. Giles has already gone down to his clinic in the cellar. His father, Asa, is at the shipping company office as usual."

"I don't remember him either."

"Once you meet him, you'll not soon forget him again. He looks like Polly. They are brother and sister. But he is taller and his disposition is more acid."

She smiled faintly. "He sounds a memorable character."

"He is. He doesn't approve of anything Giles does. In the first place, he didn't want him to be a doctor. Then he was against his marrying my sister, Olive. And now he's complaining about the experiments Giles is conducting in the consumptives' clinic he has established in the cellar."

"I can't remember anything of Giles' work either," she confessed.

"He has a visiting clinic for consumptive victims in the area and there are enough of them," Valeria said. "They come for regular checkups and treatment. And he makes notes on their cases and spends his remaining hours experimenting to find a cure for the dread disease."

"It's too bad his father is opposed to such a worthy work," Maggie commented.

The other girl made a face. "Asa is not a kind man like his son. Happily he has taken a liking to me or I don't think I could remain here."

"How does he feel about me?"

"As my friend he's made you welcome," Valeria assured her. "I can't imagine you having forgotten all these things."

"I'm sorry."

Valeria put an arm around her. "We're the ones who should be sorry. It was a most unfortunate accident."

Maggie said, "Your sister, Olive, must have been a fine person. Giles still seems shattered by her loss."

Valeria looked grave. "He was deeply in love with Olive."

"I'm sure of that."

"Her illness and death left him in a sorry state. That is why I came here."

"What sort of illness did she have?"

"A cruel, wasting disease," the dark girl said. "At first we feared it might be consumption. But Giles soon was satisfied this wasn't the case. Olive's illness was of an obscure origin and even worse. She had been beautiful but in the end she refused to see anyone."

"How awful for her!"

"Yes. And for Giles. When she finally died he buried her quickly without notifying any of her friends. The ceremony took place that very night. I remember standing by her open grave as the coffin was lowered into it. And they shoveled back the earth by the light of torches. I shall never forget the expression on Giles' face as he stood there. It was one of utter despair."

Maggie was touched. "I'm sure you must be doing him a great deal of good by staying here."

"It is a small thing," Valeria said deprecatingly.

"Who knows? Perhaps one day you two will marry."

The dark girl looked at her in surprise. "You're quite wrong in that."

"Really?"

"Yes," Valeria said with a wistful smile. "That accident really did rob you of memory of the most important things. Since you've come here to stay Giles has fallen in love with you."

She stared at the girl. "I don't believe it."

"You better had."

"But he gave me no sign of it last night," she protested.

"He is a very considerate man. Knowing you were ill, he'd give no hint of his feelings."

"This is more and more confusing," Maggie protested.

"Try not to think about it," Valeria advised. "If Giles says your memory will return gradually, depend on it that it will. And now why don't we take a walk in the sunshine?"

They did. And the tang of the sea air together with the benevolent warmth of the summer sun made Maggie feel much better. She decided that Valeria was right—she must adjust herself to the situation as best she could, and meanwhile pray that her memory would return.

The two girls strolled as far as Widows' Hill and as Maggie stood there at this familiar spot and heard the breakers below she felt somewhat less uneasy. Yet, when she stared at the distant cluster of buildings on the point of land marking the village of Collinsport, they seemed to be much smaller and less imposing than when she'd last seen them.

She turned her eyes to the stately mansion of Collinwood, which Valeria said was known as the new house. It too looked different. She was sure she remembered a sun porch on one side of it, but this was not in evidence.

Valeria said, "You are studying Collinwood. In case you've forgotten, let me warn you that it has not a happy history."

"In what way?"

"It seems to have brought misfortune to each of its succeeding owners," Valeria told her gravely. "The wife of its builder killed herself by jumping from this very cliff. And every generation of the Collins family has known some macabre sorrow."

Maggie gave the girl a startled look. "Do they say it is haunted?"

Valeria met her glance. In an even voice she asked, "Why do you bring that up?"

She hesitated, then said, "I thought I saw a ghost last night."

"What sort of ghost?" The other girl's tone was strained.

"Giles gave me a sleeping potion. I was only half awake. But I saw this figure in a loose robe with a cowl almost hiding her face. As she came closer I saw they were pink. She was bathed in pink. And when I saw her withered, crone's face, it was tinted with the same color."

"A pink ghost!"

"Yes."

Valeria looked distressed. "Perhaps it was only a nightmare."

"It must have been, I suppose. But I'm not sure. It stays with me so. I can almost see her face and form now."

Valeria said hesitantly, "There has been some strange talk lately. I have heard whispers of a ghost at Collinwood. Yet I have never seen anything out of the way."

"But others have?"

She shrugged. "The servants and a few of the villagers. But they are poor ignorant folk who like to believe in such things. Not very good witnesses, I fear."

"Then you don't think the house is haunted?"

"I don't know what to believe," Valeria said frankly. "But I wouldn't mention any of this to Giles or his father. It would only distress and perhaps anger them."

"I'll remember," she promised.

The dark girl gave her an uneasy look. "Should you see anything again I wish you'd tell me. And then maybe we can investigate it."

"I will."

They turned and walked back to the big house. Maggie

regretted having brought up the subject, as it had obviously distressed her friend. For she had already accepted the charming dark beauty in this role. And she hoped that having her close by would make the ordeal of her gradual recovery easier for her. As they neared the house she was astonished to see a motley array of people gathered in a line beside a cellar entrance to Collinwood.

Halting on the lawn, she asked, "What can be going on?"

Valeria smiled bitterly. "Giles' clinic patients for the day are waiting their turn to visit him."

"I had no idea it would be like this!" she exclaimed in awe as she noted there must be about fifteen people of all ages in the line.

"They line up in this fashion three days a week. The other three days he gives wholly to his experiments to discover a cure for the disease."

"What a wonderful person he is," Maggie said fervently.

"Yes. And his father is just his opposite. Asa Collins resents these poor souls invading the grounds and the house. On wet days Giles insists that they line up in the front hall and enter the cellar laboratory by an inside door. It has been the cause of frequent quarrels between them."

"But as a doctor, Giles must feel it his duty to help these unfortunates."

"His father berates him for not engaging in regular practice rather than restricting himself to file treatment of consumptives."

"Giles might achieve a real victory over the disease by giving it his full attention," Maggie protested.

"I agree. But Asa Collins doesn't see it that way. He claims that Giles is endangering the health of everyone in the house by allowing these sick people to come here. And the servants are terrified by the threat of the disease."

When they came close to the line of the unhappy consumptive victims she was shocked by their look of gauntness and general poverty. They all had the emaciated, hollow-cheeked appearance of the sufferers of this dread lung disease. It struck her that the line of waiting sick were fairly evenly divided between youngsters and the young middle-aged. But some were so far gone in their wasting away as to appear of advanced years.

She tried to get an impression of them without actually staring at them. And she saw that many in the somber line were giving lackluster attention to her and Valeria. An almost continual barrage of racking coughs came from the consumptives; as soon as one finished another would take up the sorry strain. Most of them wore ragged clothes and their general expression was one of utter hopelessness.

Valeria quickly guided her past the line towards the front of the great mansion. The girl said in a low tone, "I must confess that every time I see them my stomach churns. Their plight sickens me with sorrow."

"Do they come from any distance?"

"Many of them journey for miles to see the doctor," Valeria said. "Most of those who come to him are far gone with the disease. When they are only a little ill they do not bother to ask for treatment. This infuriates Giles."

They entered the cool of the big house, but Maggie was haunted by the memory of that line of unfortunates she'd seen outside. The day passed quickly enough. In the afternoon she and Valeria had tea with Aunt Polly in the rear parlor. They left only after that stout, tart-tongued old woman had dozed over her cup.

Then Maggie went up to her room to rest a little and later dress for dinner. She still felt strange in the room and was not even familiar with her wardrobe. But the closet was filled with attractive gowns and she selected a brown taffeta trimmed with lace for dinner. Her friend had warned her that old Asa Collins insisted on dining on the dot of seven and liked all the family to dress for the occasion.

Valeria had also told her something about her past. Maggie learned that she was an orphan—wealthy, as her clothes hinted—who had lived in Boston and been a close friend of Olive, Giles' late wife. Valeria had journeyed to Boston to visit her, and thinking she might make Giles a suitable wife, had invited her to Collinwood. And, Valeria concluded, Giles was already close to proposing.

It was difficult for Maggie to cope with all these revelations. How, for instance, could she respond to Giles? At present she felt nothing for him, save admiration for his medical work.

When she went downstairs the others had already gathered in the dining room. Asa Collins, tall and erect in spite of his age, stood at the head of the table to greet her. He had a sour, weathered face.

"I trust you are feeling yourself again. Miss Evans," he said gruffly.

"I'm much better," she assured him. She took a place next to Aunt Polly.

Giles Collins smiled across at her, from the opposite side of the table where he sat with Valeria beside him. "I'm sorry I didn't get a chance to see you earlier. But my patients kept me busy and I assumed you were all right or someone would have let me know."

Aunt Polly gave him an angry glance. "You should have visited her anyway. Wasting your time on that scum!"

Valeria smiled at Maggie in a way that told her she'd better get used to such arguing; there was a good deal of it at the table. Maggie spoke only when someone directly addressed her. She still felt a complete stranger among them.

At last dinner ended and they left the paneled dining room for the elegant front parlor. Giles excused himself to return to his cellar laboratory and complete work on an urgent experiment. A little later, Valeria deserted the room to find her sewing box upstairs, leaving Maggie with the two older members of the Collins clan.

From her tall-backed chair Aunt Polly observed, "Are you a regular reader of Godey's Lady's Book?"

Maggie smiled uneasily. "I don't think so."

The stout woman lifted her eyebrows. "I distinctly remember you saying that you liked it only a few days ago."

"I'm sorry. My memory."

From the fireplace where he stood, Asa Collins rasped, "Are you in accord with the ideas of President Hayes or do you not deign to interest yourself in the unladylike business of politics?"

Before she could frame any sort of reply Maggie was aware of the entry of another person in the room. She turned to see a tall, handsome dark man in a caped coat standing in the doorway of the parlor. At once she jumped to her feet. "Barnabas!" She hurried over to him. For she had at last remembered one person in Barnabas Collins!

CHAPTER 3

Barnabas Collins greeted her with a smile. "I'm glad to see you on your feet and looking so well," he said. "I'd been told that Raven threw you from the saddle and you were badly injured."

"I did take a bad fall," she agreed. "In fact, my memory is still playing tricks on me. That is why it is so encouraging that I knew you."

Barnabas raised his eyebrows. "Does Giles know about this memory loss you've suffered?"

"Yes. And he promises I'll gradually remember."

"I should certainly hope so," Barnabas said with concern.

Asa Collins had come down the length of the room to stand by them. The tall, sour man's lip was curled derisively. "It seems you must have made a much more favorable impression on this young lady than the rest of us, Barnabas," he said. "You're the only one she's recognized."

His handsome face showed a mocking expression. "I can only reply that I am grateful."

From her chair, Aunt Polly remarked tartly, "Our British cousin is always a favorite with the ladies, it seems. How are you making out in the old house, Barnabas?"

"Very well," he said in his courtly way. "Mrs. Judd and Letty have made the place very comfortable."

"Indeed," Aunt Polly said primly, her chubby hands folded in her lap. "I have heard some strange talk about those two."

"They are both very fine ladies," Barnabas responded smoothly.

Asa eyed him coldly. "We've heard other stories. How long do you plan to be here, Barnabas?"

He traced the silver wolf's head of his cane with one finger. "I don't know. I hadn't realized there was a limit to my welcome here."

"There could be," Asa said in an icy tone. "I wouldn't plan a lengthy stay."

"I'll remember that," Barnabas said quietly. And turning to Maggie, he suggested, "Let's take a short walk together. It's a lovely moonlight night."

"I'd like to," she said enthusiastically, eager to get away and talk to Barnabas privately.

Aunt Polly was on her feet now. "I don't think you should go," she said. "It strikes me you're overdoing it. You should be in your bed resting."

"I'll just go for a short walk."

The old woman frowned in annoyance. "It seems you young people must have your own way. Then let it be on your head, whatever happens."

Maggie said goodnight and hurried out of the mansion with Barnabas. Not until they were a distance from Collinwood did she relax a little.

Looking up into the handsome face beside her, she said, "I had to get out of there. I don't understand them at all. And why were they so mean to you?"

Barnabas smiled wanly. "They are difficult people, my dear, almost as suspicious and ignorant as the most deprived of the villagers. They don't understand me, so they fear me."

"But why?"

They had come to a bench in the garden and he paused for her to sit down and then he sat beside her. His strong, sad face appeared pale in the moonlight as he stared out at the moonlit ocean. Speaking in a dreamy, hypnotic fashion, he said, "It's a long story. Much too long to repeat here. But I had the urge to return here to the home of my ancestors. Letty is the daughter of a friend of mine who was killed in a railway disaster and Mrs. Judd is her grandmother. The two travel with me and take charge of my household affairs. I believe there have been ugly stories in the village concerning Mrs. Judd. People claim she is a witch and in league with the Devil."

"What ridiculous talk!" Maggie exclaimed. "Why should they say such things?"

He gave her one of his sad smiles. "They have misinterpreted some of her actions," he said. "And she has the look of a witch, I must admit. But she is actually a rather harmless old lady who enjoys walking about in graveyards late at night—a truly strange pastime, but one that does others no harm."

"That should be explained to them."

"It's rather difficult to argue with the superstitious," Barnabas said. "They have whispered about me as well, chiefly because I rarely leave the house in the daytime. I happen to have things to occupy me in the daylight hours, but they do not accept that. They prefer to put my behavior down to some dark and devious weakness. And they even have dubbed Letty, a truly lovely young woman, as a temptress also in league with the demons. It would be amusing under other circumstances."

"But Asa Collins and his sister seem to take it all very seriously," she pointed out.

"I know." He sighed. "So it is likely I shall soon say goodbye to Collinwood."

"Please don't go!" she begged him, reaching out and touching his hand. And she was at once startled by its coldness. "Your hand has a clammy chill to it," she said. "Are you feeling ill?"

"Merely weariness," he told her. "When I am very tired they become cold and numb."

"If you go I'll be completely lost here," she told him. "I don't feel easy with any of them."

"Not even with my cousin, Dr. Giles?"

"Better with him, but I'm not completely relaxed with him either."

"Yet you recognized me at once."

She nodded. "Yes. But I must admit I've no remembrance of this Mrs. Judd or the Letty you speak of. My mind is so muddled. But it seems to me you have a manservant."

"I'm afraid you're wrong there," he said in his good-natured way. "It would be better for all concerned if that was the case, with the villagers accusing me of harboring a witch."

She glanced back at Collinwood looming darkly against the moonlit sky. Small yellow squares of light showed from a few of its windows. She gave a tiny shudder.

"I don't know," she said. "Suddenly I'm terrified of remaining at Collinwood."

"Understandable," Barnabas said quietly.

"What do you mean?"

"You are a sensitive young woman," he said. "Things there are not as they seem. They offer a facade for more evil than you can imagine. You feel this evil."

She stared up at his solemn, handsome face with a kind of

awe. "That is so close to the truth, I'm terrified," she confessed. "What kind of evil are you talking about?"

Barnabas frowned. "I'd better not reveal any more to you at this time. But I had to warn you, put you on the alert for the unexpected and the frightening."

"Something is very wrong in Collinwood," she agreed. "Has it to do with the death of Giles' wife? Didn't she suffer from some unknown, hideous disease?"

"I believe so."

"And he's still haunted by the memory of her death. Yet Valeria claims he's fallen in love with me."

Barnabas looked at her steadily for a moment. "You would do well not to take that young woman too seriously either."

"You can't mean she's in any way a part of this evil you mention?"

He shrugged. "I'm telling you she may not turn out to be the close friend she pretends. Just be careful with her."

Concern flooded Maggie's pretty face. "Why did this have to happen? I feel as if I'd awakened to a dreadful nightmare . . . a nightmare in which you and this place are all that I recognize."

He touched a comforting hand to her shoulder. "I'm sorry, I should not have spoken so frankly. I'd forgotten about your accident for the moment. You mustn't worry. I believe you'll be completely safe for a while."

"I'll not ever feel right until I have regained my memory and am able to sort things out for myself," she worried.

"There's no need to panic. I'm always close by."

"But Asa ordered you to leave," she reminded him. "And it won't take much longer for his patience to run out. Then I'll be alone."

"Asa often says more than he means," Barnabas explained. "He'll get over his anger at me and forget about telling me to go. Depend on it."

"I need to," she confessed. After a moment's pause, she continued, "I believe a ghost came into my room last night. A ghost all in pink."

"A pink ghost?"

"Yes," she nodded, her eyes wide with fear. "It came close to my bed. I could see its horrible face. An old, withered face contorted with hatred. I screamed and then the thing vanished."

Barnabas was frowning. "Have you told this story to anyone else?"

"Yes."

"Who?"

"Valeria," she said. "Did I do wrong?"

"Perhaps," Barnabas told her. "At any rate, I wouldn't mention any other such visitations to her. I'd rather you confided only in me. I may be able to help."

"Do you think it really was a ghost?"

He glanced over his shoulder at the old mansion. "Collinwood has many of them."

"What will I do?"

He turned to her again. "Have faith in me," he said. "And don't listen to any gossip you may hear about me. Also, don't confide too much in Valeria or any of the others in the house."

"Not even Giles?"

"Not even Giles," he said firmly. Then he stood up and once again she was impressed by how tall and broad-shouldered he was. If it were not for the sallow color of his skin he would be truly handsome, and even that did not rob him of charm.

She clung to him. "I wish you were living in the new house."

Barnabas held her in his arms. "The old one is best suited to my needs," he told her. "If you are ever frightened in the night send a message to me. Rouse one of the maids or the workmen on the estate. Get them to carry your message to me."

"I hope I'm not bothered again."

"And so do I," he agreed as he kissed her gently on the forehead. And again she was strangely bothered by the coldness of his lips. He said, "I must get you back to the house at once. They'll be certain I've harmed you in some way."

Reluctantly she allowed him to escort her back. They walked swiftly through the phantom daylight of the silver moon. When they were a short distance from the entrance steps to the grim mansion he paused. "I'll leave you here."

"When will I see you again?"

"Soon."

"Why can't we meet in the daytime?" she wanted to know. "There are so many things I want to discuss with you."

"I'm sorry," he said, a veiled expression transforming his face. "I have serious matters to occupy me in the daylight hours. You must be content with our meetings after dusk."

There was a finality in his manner that did not encourage further discussion. They said goodnight and she moved slowly towards the door of Collinwood. Even before she entered, she was trembling slightly.

She opened the door and stepped into the dimly lighted entrance hall. Standing there with an angry look on his pale sensitive face was Dr. Giles Collins.

"So you were out there with Barnabas," he said accusingly.

She gazed at his angry face with disbelief. "Yes," she admitted,

"I was. Is there anything wrong in that?"

"Need you ask me?"

"I don't understand you," she exclaimed, with a tremor of fear in her voice.

The young doctor gripped her fiercely by the arms. In a tense voice he demanded, "How could you do this to me, knowing the way I feel about you?"

Thoroughly bewildered and increasingly afraid, she asked, "Why shouldn't I take a walk with Barnabas if I want?"

"He is not fit company for any young girl!"

"That's not true!" she exclaimed. "Please let me go!"

"Not yet," Giles said firmly, the cold look on his face now reminding her of his father's dour countenance. She began to wonder if there wasn't a lot of Asa Collins in this son after all. He went on, "You know that I'm in love with you, that I want you to marry me!"

"Let's not talk about that now," she pleaded.

"I must," he said. "Barnabas is an evil man. You haven't heard the stories about him. That he stalks and attacks young girls in the village lanes. Our maids are afraid to go out after dark."

"I don't believe it!"

"It's true," Giles went on. "That is why my father wants him to give up tenancy of the old house—him and the two creatures he has with him. One of them is a wanton beauty and the other a bent crone. And both of them in league with the Devil, the same as he is, if the stories told are true!"

"If the stories told are true!" she repeated scornfully. "Well, I don't care to hear or believe them."

He stared at her incredulously, the anger draining out of his face and his expression becoming one of despair. He released his hold on her arms and stood there abjectly.

"What can I say to make you keep away from him?"

"Nothing you say can change my opinion of Barnabas. I like him."

He nodded sadly. "Very well. Then you will have to learn the truth for yourself."

"I'm sure that would be the better way," she said defiantly. "And now I'd like to go up to my room. I'm very tired."

"Maggie, forgive me!" the young doctor begged. "I was so jealous I completely forgot about your accident. I had no right to behave as I did with you in such a state."

"It's unfortunate you didn't think of that earlier."

Giles still continued to block her way to the stairs. "I deserve your condemnation," he agreed. "But please see my side of it. I discover you are out with the charming but unprincipled Barnabas. I love you. I'm also very weary from a long day and evening in my laboratory. I haven't even fully recovered from the loss of my wife yet. Try to understand."

His despairing plea made her anger fade. She gazed at his pale, anxious face and couldn't help feeling sorry for him. Jealousy was all too common a weakness. And he had suffered a great deal, not to mention that he'd worn himself out trying to cure the victims of consumption in the area.

Quietly, she told him, "I'll not hold it against you."

"Thank you, Maggie." He touched her arm with great gentleness.

She lowered her eyes. "And now please let me go upstairs."

"I'll do better than that," he promised. "I'll see you to the door of your room."

"There's no need."

"But I will," he insisted. "Valeria was greatly distressed when she learned where you had gone and in whose company. I promised her I would see you safely upstairs."

It hardly seemed worth debating.

"If you like," she said with a note of resignation in her voice. "You should be resting, yourself."

"I intend to go straight to bed after I leave you," he assured her as they started up the broad stairway.

"It's a beautiful night," she remarked by way of staving off the awkwardness that had come between them.

"I know."

They had reached the first landing. There was only a small lamp with a badly-smoked shade to offer a murky light from its wall bracket mounting. They went down the shadowed hallway and took a second stairway. The young doctor at her side appeared to be as tense as she was.

There was no light at all in the upper hall. She was suddenly grateful that Giles was at her side. They'd only gone a few steps down the hall toward her room when she came to a frozen halt. Ahead of them, at the very end of the hallway, the phantom in pink suddenly loomed out of the darkness and then merged with the shadows once again.

"Look!" she cried in a startled voice and pointed.

Giles stared down the hallway. "What is it?"

"Didn't you see?" She searched his face in urgent disbelief.

"See what?"

"Don't pretend. The ghost! I saw her!"

"Maggie, what are you talking about?" he demanded. "There was nothing. I didn't see a thing."

"But I pointed her out to you."

"I saw you pointing to the end of the corridor," he admitted.

"But I didn't see anything else and I'm positive you didn't either. It has to be your imagination!"

"Has to be?" she demanded. "I'm sorry. But I did see the phantom, all in pink just the same as before. And I won't be talked out of it."

He seemed thoroughly shaken by her obstinance. "I don't understand this, Maggie," he said unhappily, "but let's not argue about it anymore."

"Just as you say," she told him. "But there is a ghost here."

He smiled bleakly. "Every old mansion is supposed to be haunted."

"This one is."

"You're the first one I've known to claim to have seen a spirit here," he said as they went on down to her door.

Her hand on the knob, she said, "Thank you for your company."

He gave her a pleading look in the shadows. "Don't hate me, Maggie."

"I don't," she said in a quiet voice.

He took her in his arms for a brief kiss before leaving. She quickly let herself into her own room, relieved that her bed was turned down as it had been the night before, and that the lamp was glowing faintly on her bedside table. She closed the door behind her and bolted it.

The moonlight was showing through her window and she couldn't help wondering if Barnabas was still out there alone somewhere. Remembering the veiled warning Barnabas had given her about the young doctor and the others in the house, it struck her odd that both men should have spoken of each other in such a dark manner.

All it did was add to her confusion, just as this latest incident in the hall had. No one would ever convince her that she hadn't seen the phantom in pink again. Yet when she'd pointed the ghostly figure out to Giles, he'd pretended he couldn't see it. Or had he really not seen it?

Was the apparition visible to her eyes only? Did the eerie figure in pink have a special message for her? Did this have something to do with the accident? If only she could remember! She was certain she somehow had learned the answers to all that was happening to her here now. Hadn't she, at some earlier time, discussed Giles Collins and Valeria Norris with Barnabas? It was a blur to her. She had lost the link of memory and this left her a helpless victim of events.

Barnabas Collins seemed to be her only hope. He knew a great deal more than he cared to reveal to her; he had admitted as much tonight.

According to what she'd been told it was only after she'd come to Collinwood as a guest that she'd met Barnabas. So why should she have this conviction that she'd known him before meeting any of the others?

Slowly she changed for the night, thinking almost against her will of the things that Giles had said to her. He'd hinted that Barnabas had been suspected of attacking some of the village girls. She couldn't imagine the handsome man in such a role; surely she had always found Barnabas a complete gentleman. But the rumors must be founded on some small basis of fact.

Barnabas had mentioned that his elderly housekeeper, Mrs. Judd, prowled in cemeteries in the dark hours and because of this had been dubbed a witch by the villagers. No doubt some equally minor violation of the ordinary had caused the ignorant and superstitious to brand Barnabas a menace.

She intended to discuss this matter with him and hear his side of it. She felt sure he would offer her a reasonable explanation. As she buttoned the throat of her nightgown, ready to get in bed, she hesitated before the bedside table on which the lamp rested. Should she extinguish its flame and depend on the bright moonlight to illuminate her bedchamber?

Glancing towards the windows, she saw that it was still radiantly silver outside and made up her mind to do without the lamp. Removing its decorated shade, she turned down the wick and then blew out the flame. Its absence made little difference in the room. After returning the shade to its place she sat on the side of the bed.

It was then that the high-pitched scream, a shrill feminine cry of terror, reached her with shocking clarity from the grounds below. A surge of chilling fear went through Maggie as she hurried across to the window. It seemed to her that the frantic scream had come from the front of the old mansion.

Now she strained to see some sign of a figure on the lawns. But there was no one. A series of hedges divided the lawns and gardens and she tried especially to spot someone seeking concealment in the shadow of these barriers. But the grounds appeared deserted.

Minutes had passed since the scream, but her eyes remained fixed on the grounds bathed in the weird silver of the moonlight. Then she gasped. A figure strode quickly across the most distant section of the broad lawns. Barnabas Collins!

There was no mistaking the erect figure in the caped coat. He seemed to be making his way towards the path that led to the old house. She watched as he quickly turned the corner of the house and was lost to her view.

A moment later she heard hoarse male shouts. And then two men came into sight, apparently on the trail of Barnabas. They were taking the same route across the grounds and talking loudly, although she was unable to make out what they were saying.

A sickening feeling of apprehension filled her. She dared not try to imagine what had happened. But the scream must in some way be linked with the appearance of Barnabas out there, and the men following him were obviously convinced he was guilty of some crime. What had Barnabas done to cause this midnight alarm?

Maggie remained at the window for what seemed an endless time. Then the two men came walking back. They were moving more slowly now and their voices had dropped as if the chase and excitement had come to an end.

She gave a deep sigh of relief. Judging by what she'd seen, Barnabas had managed to elude his pursuers. And since she doubted very much that he had been guilty of any misdemeanor, she was glad to know that he had gotten safely away.

As the two men retreated across the lawn what seemed to be a large black bird came winging through the air to hover a distance above them. The men were at once aware of its presence and halted to gaze up at it. Maggie watched fascinated for at least a minute before she realized it wasn't a bird but a giant bat.

She'd always had a deep revulsion for bats, and the size of this one gave her a feeling of terror. It ended its hovering above the two men to swiftly wing higher in the air and darted toward the window where she was standing.

She stumbled back with a tiny cry of fear, certain that it would shatter the glass and be upon her.

But as the bat came perilously close to the window it again shifted direction and flew straight out toward the cliff and the sea. She watched after it until it was only a tiny speck and then vanished altogether. Not until then did she realize perspiration had broken out at her temples and she was trembling.

She quickly left the window and returned to her bed. Her troubled thoughts made sleep long in coming—and then, of course, dreams tormented her. The climax came as a harsh voice whispered in her ear, "You are the one! You are the one!"

The words cut so vividly into her consciousness that she awoke with a start to gaze around her in the moonlit room. But there was no one in sight. It had been a phantom voice of her dreams, she decided.

CHAPTER 4

The following morning was sunny and warm again. In spite of the previous night's events, Maggie was feeling better. Yet her memory was still as obscured as ever. She wondered if the others had heard the screams from the lawn that had shaken her and if Barnabas had been linked with the happenings in any way.

As soon as she had breakfasted she went downstairs. When she reached the first landing she heard voices in the entrance hallway and looking down, saw Valeria Norris in earnest conversation with an elderly man with gray mutton-chop whiskers. The man was dressed in brown tweeds and carried his hat in his hand, revealing a bald head. His tone was servile as he addressed the pretty dark girl. Maggie, waiting with her hand on the bannister, could not help overhearing what was being said.

"It's not an easy business to look into, Miss Norris."

"I understand that."

The man shifted his weight from foot to foot uneasily. "After all, we don't have any reliable witnesses. And Mr. Barnabas is Dr. Collins' cousin and I doubt if he'd want any trouble that wasn't necessary."

"Dr. Collins wants justice done," Valeria said in a firm voice. "And he does not expect special treatment for his cousin."

"Granting that, I just don't have enough to go on."

"I think you have. But then, that is bound to be a matter of opinion."

The bald man gazed at his shoes. "If I could have a few words with the doctor."

"I'm afraid that is quite impossible this morning," Valeria responded coldly. "The doctor is expecting patients for the clinic at noon. And he is busy preparing for them."

"Well, then, I'd better go and come back another time," the bald man suggested.

"I trust you are not going to treat this matter in a dilatory fashion. Constable Withers," Valeria said sharply.

"Depend on that, miss," he replied uneasily.

"If Barnabas Collins is the culprit we want him punished," Valeria went on. "There must be no partiality because he happens to be a guest here and a member of the family. Dr. Collins would not want that."

Withers nodded. "I fully understand, miss."

"I hope you do, Constable," Valeria said in an icy tone. "These incidents must end, no matter who suffers."

"Yes, miss." The constable was edging towards the door.

Valeria followed him. "Mr. Asa Collins is not as temperate as his son, Constable. And he has lately expressed himself as dissatisfied with the way you are carrying out your duties. I warn you of this since he is quite capable of trying to have you removed from office."

Constable Withers halted by the door indignantly. His face had become florid.

In a quiet voice, he told the girl, "There would be some others in the village have a word to say about that, miss. Not a soul in Collinsport can point a finger at me and claim I have neglected my duty."

Valeria at once took a different attitude. "Please don't misunderstand me, Constable. I merely told you that for your own good. I didn't mean to imply that Mr. Asa Collins had any intention of causing you trouble. It is just that all of us at Collinwood are concerned and fearful of what has been going on."

"Yes, miss," the Constable said with simple dignity. "I'll call back later to talk with Dr. Collins."

Maggie continued to wait at the head of the stairway as the dark girl saw the constable out. She had no intention of letting Valeria know she'd overheard the conversation between her and the constable. For some reason the girl had seemed determined to have Barnabas prosecuted; but she had defeated her purpose by pressing the matter so arrogantly.

As Valeria came back into the entrance hall Maggie made

her way down the stairs.

Valeria greeted her with a nod and a look of interest. "You seem so much better this morning."

Maggie was at the bottom step. "I feel better."

"I've just been talking to the constable."

"Oh?"

"Did you hear any commotion last night?"

"I thought I heard a girl scream. It must have been around midnight."

"You did," Valeria said with a grim look. "That is why we summoned the constable. But I'm afraid he hasn't been much help. Giles should have talked with him but he had to go straight down to the laboratory this morning. It is to be one of his busy days."

Maggie pretended innocence. "You say you called on the constable because of last night. What exactly happened?"

Valeria sighed. "It's rather a long story. If you'll come with me to the conservatory I'll tell you. I think we should go there. Otherwise, Aunt Polly or someone is liable to interrupt us."

Maggie followed her along the hall to the rear of the house where the glass-walled room filled with plants was located. The air was stifling; Maggie wished that Valeria had suggested they have their discussion outside. It would have been much more pleasant and just as private.

Valeria went the length of the room and turned to continue the conversation. She gave her a meaningful look as she confided, "Last night one of the maids here was attacked."

"That was who I heard?"

"Yes. She'd spent the evening with her young man. He saw her as far as the barns and left her to walk the rest of the short distance to the house. It was then she was pounced on in the darkness."

"Was she able to recognize her attacker?"

Valeria looked grim. "She has babbled a lot of nonsense so that she thoroughly confused Constable Withers . . . but from her description I would say that it was Barnabas."

Maggie frowned. "I can't believe that!"

"None of us want to believe it," was Valeria's comment, "but everything points to him."

"Was the girl sure?"

"No. That's what makes it so annoying. You'd think she'd have a clear impression of who it was. But the girl's brain seems to have been addled by the shock. After giving what I'd call a perfect description of Barnabas, she began to rave about a bat coming after her and biting her on the neck. And there is a red mark on her throat."

Maggie was all attention. "Perhaps it's true. I, too, saw a huge bat in flight last night."

"Did you?" Valeria sounded dubious.

"Yes, I went to the window right after I heard the scream." Valeria was studying her keenly. "Was that all you saw?"

"Why do you ask?"

"Because the gardener and his son heard the maid's screams and went to her rescue. By the time they got there they only caught a glimpse of a tall, well-built man resembling Barnabas hurrying across the lawn. They gave chase but he eluded them. And a few minutes later they also saw this mysterious large bat. It hovered above them before heading out in the direction of the ocean."

Maggie had no intention of offering evidence against Barnabas. And after all, she couldn't be positive it was he she'd seen. It could have been a complete stranger. Carefully she said, "In the darkness it was hard to see."

"There was moonlight."

"I still could not see clearly."

Valeria looked unconvinced. "How unfortunate," she said. "I was hoping you'd seen Barnabas and been able to positively identify him for us."

"Even then, that wouldn't prove he was the one who had attacked the maid."

Valeria looked annoyed. "It would surely be evidence enough."

"I rather doubt it."

"I think it is time you knew the gossip that is being retailed here by the local folk. They believe Barnabas has set up some kind of black magic circle in the old house. And they are blaming Giles and his father for renting Barnabas the house."

"That sounds childish," she remonstrated.

"I'm not so sure," Valeria said with that icy glint in her black eyes again. "The talk goes that Mrs. Judd is a witch. They also claim that Barnabas is a vampire and that Letty, the young blonde, is his consort."

Maggie gasped. "You surely don't condone such talk?"

"Naturally not," Valeria said. "Barnabas is a Collins and the family doesn't want any needless scandal. But Giles is worried. It was an ancestor of Barnabas, the first Barnabas Collins, who left here almost a hundred years ago under the cloud of being a vampire."

"I don't believe such things as vampires exist," Maggie argued.

Valeria spread her hands. "Think what you like. It is all in the family journals. The first Barnabas Collins departed from

Collinwood in disgrace. And who can say that this descendant of his does not bear the same taint?"

"Barnabas Collins is a charming man and my friend," Maggie told her. "I don't like to hear such things said about him."

Valeria's lovely face mirrored her troubled frame of mind. "The girl last night was not the first one to be attacked. There have been others. And all of them have had the same red marks on their throats that I found on her throat this morning. The kiss of the vampire!"

"Why would he do such a thing?"

"To maintain his life," she said calmly. "Those living under the vampire curse must have human blood for sustenance or they wither and perish. If Barnabas is truly one of the walking dead that explains why he is seen only at night and why he attacks these young girls to drink their blood."

She shook her head. "It's too fantastic."

"Yet it is the pattern of the vampire. And who knows what evil those other two may be up to? Several times I have found that Mrs. Judd lurking near the house. She might be casting a spell on us all!"

Maggie was shocked. "You speak of her as if she really were a witch!"

"She well could be," Valeria said. "I'm beginning to regret that I ever invited you here. I fear we may all be in for some bad times."

"If I could only think clearly," Maggie said with a frown.

"Your memory is still a blank?"

"For most things. I did recognize Barnabas and call him by name."

Valeria eyed her bleakly. "That only goes to show he does have some strange powers. Otherwise, why should he have so impressed himself on your mind?"

"I don't think that's being fair to him."

"Think what you like," she said. "We are all in trouble."

"Perhaps I should leave then."

Valeria at once changed in her manner. "No, I do not believe that would be any solution," she said. "It would be foolhardy for you to try to return to Boston in your present condition."

"I warn you if I remain I shall continue to be sympathetic to Barnabas."

Valeria forced a smile. "I'll not try to make up your mind on that score," she said. "As a guest here you are entitled to your own opinions. I have warned you what is being said about Barnabas. I felt I owed you that."

"Thank you."

"And do not forget the appearance of your phantom in pink," her friend reminded her. "That has not been explained."

"I hardly expect it to be," Maggie said, anxious to get away from the overpowering heat of the conservatory. The tall green plants around her actually seemed to be greedily pressing towards her. If she did not soon escape from the hot-house atmosphere and Valeria's monstrous accusations, she would faint.

"I'd think about that if I were you. I wouldn't be surprised if Barnabas could give you some hint as to the identity of your phantom."

"Is that all?" Maggie asked her. "I'm stifling in here. I must get out into the fresh air."

Valeria stood there framed by the exotic plants. She smiled thinly. "Don't let me detain you," she said. "I've told you everything I wanted to."

And more than enough, Maggie thought grimly. She turned and hurriedly sought her way out of the plant-cluttered glass room. The cool of the hallway was a relief but she did not stop until she had stepped out the front door and descended into the rose garden.

She stood there, the slight breeze ruffling her dark hair a little, her eyes on the distant cliffs, and tried to sort out her feelings. Only last night Barnabas had warned her of evil lurking behind the placid facade of Collinwood. She had not guessed then that a good deal of this evil would be directed against him. Why was Valeria so anxious to point the finger of guilt at Barnabas? And Giles must be a party to this as well.

After her experience with the young doctor last night she no longer admired him quite so much, nor was she so sure of his kindly nature. For a brief period he had shown himself to be cruel and unrelenting. What did these two have against Barnabas?

The most obvious answer was that the handsome English cousin of the Collins family might be everything they claimed he was. Perhaps such examples of the living dead did walk the earth. Yet she found it difficult to associate Barnabas with such morbid creatures. She was sure Valeria and Giles were prejudiced and wrong.

There was another possibility. Perhaps Valeria was in love with the tall, handsome visitor and angry because he showed no romantic interest in her. Valeria might be jealous of the blonde beauty, Letty, of whom Barnabas had spoken so warmly and who was one of his traveling companions. But this did not explain the hatred Giles also showed towards Barnabas.

A footstep on the gravel path behind her made her aware she was no longer alone. She turned to see Aunt Polly, carrying a flower basket and wearing a wide-brimmed straw hat to protect her from the sun as well as white gloves that reached to her elbows. In the basket were a pair of pruning scissors.

"Are you as fond of roses as I am?" the old woman wanted to know as she studied her with an interested expression on her wrinkled face.

"I do like them."

"I have come to get some for the house," Aunt Polly informed her. "I used to take complete care of this section of the garden but now I'm too old."

"Still, you must get a lot of pleasure from the flowers."

"I do," Aunt Polly said, moving on to inspect the nearest bushes. "Did you rest well last night?"

"Very well."

"You've probably heard that something rather unpleasant happened."

Maggie nodded. "Yes, I have."

"I don't know what it's all coming to," Aunt Polly complained as she snipped off several long-stemmed roses and placed them in the basket. "Things have been getting steadily worse at Collinwood since Olive's death."

"Really?"

The stout woman turned to her. "Giles hasn't been the same since he lost Olive. And her burial was a scandal. No one was allowed to see her for weeks before she died. He didn't even let me look at her the night of her death. Instead he had her placed in a casket and whisked off to the family cemetery to be buried by torchlight."

"I understand it was because she had failed a great deal," Maggie said softly. "He didn't want to let anyone view her in the ugliness of her illness."

Aunt Polly glanced around furtively and then bent close to Maggie. "You mustn't tell anyone, but I did get a quick glimpse of her shortly before she died. About a week before. Her room door was open a litde and I saw her standing staring out the window."

"Had she changed a great deal?"

"Faded and withered," the old woman said in a hushed tone. "And it happened in such a short time. I just stood there; I couldn't believe what I saw. Then I heard someone coming and I hurried and hid in the shadows of my doorway. It was Giles. He went into the room and closed the door without ever seeing me."

Maggie frowned. "I should think he would know what disease she was suffering from. After all, he is a doctor."

Aunt Polly smiled sourly. "If he knew, he didn't let on. My guess is that it was no ordinary illness at all."

"What do you mean?"

"I say it was a curse—a curse put upon her family. And one day Valeria will die from it, too!"

For a moment Maggie stared into Aunt Polly's glittering eyes. Was she mad? "You surely don't believe in such superstitious nonsense!"

Aunt Polly had moved back to the rose bushes again and was calmly snipping off some more blooms for her basket. "It's not nonsense. I heard Giles and Valeria talking about it."

"Isn't it likely you heard what they were saying wrong?" Maggie's tone was elaborately polite and reasonable.

Aunt Polly regarded her sarcastically over her shoulder. "I'm not daft!" she said. "I heard Valeria tell Giles it was a curse put upon her family. And he said he could do nothing about it. And then she told him he must find a way."

"That could have meant anything. People often refer to an illness as a curse. And since Giles is a doctor, naturally Valeria would beg him to do something for her sister. And it would be the expected thing for him to be discouraged."

The old woman gave a sharp cackle of laughter. "You think you're so smart. Perhaps you can explain why Valeria didn't try to marry Giles after her sister's death. She thinks enough of him. And I'm sure Giles is fond of her."

"I wouldn't know," Maggie said uneasily.

"And then Valeria brought you here and encouraged Giles to fall in love with you. Doesn't that strike you as strange?"

"I can't remember anything about my arrival here," she complained. "If I could, I might be able to answer many questions."

"It wouldn't make any difference," Aunt Polly told her enigmatically. "Valeria doesn't want to marry Giles because of the curse."

The conviction in the old woman's tone left Maggie rather shaken. The one thing she could see clearly in this dark tale was that it would be useless to try to change Aunt Polly's opinion. So she said, "I'm only a stranger here. I can't be expected to know what is going on to the extent you and the others do."

Aunt Polly's eyes glittered malevolently. "Barnabas is mad and so is Giles. And Valeria is filled to the brim with venom. I know she hates Asa and me. She and Giles would get rid of us if they dared."

"I'm sure you're wrong about all those things," Maggie said, appalled by the old woman's intensity.

"Little you know!"

Maggie had heard more than enough. Now convinced that Aunt Polly was mentally unbalanced, she quickly left the rose garden and began walking across the lawn. It was frightening how opposed to each other the various members of the household were.

Belatedly she realized she was taking the same path that she'd seen Barnabas use the night before. Well, she would go to the old house to talk to him. He had asked her not to do this, of course, explaining that he was busy with his research during the day. But she was sure he would understand and forgive her when she let him know what a strange morning she had endured.

As she rounded the corner of the house she was suddenly confronted by the waiting line of consumptives ready for their turn to be examined by Giles in his cellar clinic.

It could well have been the same group she'd seen the previous day, forlorn, hollow-cheeked and ragged.

Dull eyes focused on her as she veered a little to outflank the line. Children whined as they clutched their parents' hands, and there was the usual choir of hacking coughs. As Maggie passed the end of the line she came upon a tall, gaunt man with a stubble of beard on his cadaverous face arguing with a pale, ragged girl who stood nervously at the rear of the others.

"You will come home with me!" The gaunt man dragged at the girl's arm.

"No!" the young woman said tearfully. "I'm going to see the doctor.'"

"He will do you no good!"

Maggie felt she could not go on without trying to help the girl. She went up between them and told the man, "You really should allow her to visit Dr. Collins."

With a hacking cough he turned his wrath on her, to the amusement of those in the line. "Well, Miss High-and- Mighty, so you want to interfere? My daughter will do as I tell her!"

Maggie glanced at the sick, frightened girl. "I'd like to see your daughter helped by the doctor."

The man laughed nastily and coughed again. Pointing to Collinwood with a bony finger, he asked, "Do you truly think that villain will help her?"

"You're mistaken," she said. "Dr. Collins is a kind and competent physician."

"So you think," the thin, ragged man sneered at her. "But I know what he did to my son, Ben."

"I can't imagine him harming your son."

"That shows how little you know. Him and his experiments! You don't know what goes on in that cellar, miss!"

"I know Dr. Collins is trying to find a cure for consumption and giving of his talents to aid any sufferers in this area."

"You can't cure the consumption," the thin man said with another of his wracking coughs. "It's run through all my family.

Took my missus, then the baby and next it was Ben. Now it's got Annie here and me. There ain't nothing can help us."

"You're very wrong," she said quietly. "Even if you refuse help for yourself you should give this girl a chance."

"Send her to him? To make an old woman of her same as he made an old man of my boy, Ben. I won't have him giving his evil doses to any more of my kin. I saw Ben change from a boy into a withered old man and I know it was what the doc gave him that done it!"

"That couldn't be!" she protested.

"I know," the man said firmly. "Better to die a natural death from the consumption than to let him experiment on you. We all know what he did to his poor wife and how he covered up his deviltry by burying her at night." Turning to his daughter, he said, "Come, girl!" And he dragged her away with him.

There was a loud murmuring from the rest of the line; then two or three others left. Maggie stared at their drooping, forlorn figures retreating and wondered what madness had taken hold of them.

It was no surprise that there were those wicked rumors about Barnabas Collins and the two women of his household, considering the ignorance and superstition of the villagers. It sickened her. Without glancing at the line again she moved on.

Passing the barns and other outbuildings, she soon arrived at the old house. It looked deserted, but she felt sure Barnabas would be inside. So she went over and mounted the several steps to knock on the stout oaken door.

For a long moment there was no indication that her knocking had been heard. Then there was the sound of shuffling footsteps approaching the door from the other side. And the door swung open to reveal the bent figure of an old woman peering out at her. Maggie took one look at the thin, wizened face and was unable to stifle a gasp. It was the face of the phantom in pink!

CHAPTER 5

"Why have you come here?"

It was only when the bent figure in the doorway spoke that the spell was broken for Maggie. This was not the phantom, merely an old hag with a similar thin and wrinkled face.

"I'd like to speak to Barnabas Collins."

The old woman, whom she took to be Mrs. Judd, closed the door a little. "He is not here."

"But I know he must be," she insisted. "And I'm sure he'll be willing to see me."

"Barnabas sees no one during the day," Mrs. Judd snapped. "If you were truly a friend of his you would know that."

"Tell him it is Maggie Evans."

The door closed another inch or two, so that the wrinkled crone was peering at her through a narrow opening now. "Come back in the evening."

"But I'd like to talk with him now," Maggie said, trying to make her understand. "It's important for him as well as me."

Mrs. Judd's smile revealed sunken, toothless gums. "Next you'll be telling me he asked you to come here and see him in the afternoon. It won't do, young miss!"

"At least let him know I'm here," she pleaded. "I'll wait until you bring back his answer."

The crone cackled. "There'll be no message and no answer. Be satisfied with that."

She slammed the door. Maggie stood there a moment in consternation. It appeared getting through to Barnabas was going to be a hopeless task. With a sigh she turned and went down the steps.

She was about to start back to the new house when she happened to glance in the direction of the cemetery and saw the figure of a slim, young woman coming across the field. The girl was blonde and attractive; this had to be Letty. Hope returned to her. Surely the girl would take her message to Barnabas. And she walked down the slope to the field to meet her.

When they came face to face she saw that the blonde was truly a beauty with the delicate white skin seldom seen in any but English women. And so it was no surprise that when the girl spoke she had the same British accent as Barnabas and the ancient Mrs. Judd.

The girl said, "Who are you?"

"My name is Maggie Evans."

The girl's blue eyes showed interest. "Yes," she said. "Barnabas has told me about you. What are you doing here at this time of day?"

"I wanted to see him."

Letty gave her an almost pitying look. "Didn't he tell you that would never be possible?"

She shook her head. "I don't think so. I don't know! But I do want to see him badly. There are things I need to warn him about."

The blonde smiled wisely. "There is nothing you can tell him that he doesn't already know."

"I'm sure Valeria and Giles Collins are in league against him," she went on breathlessly. "They have even tried to enlist the constable on their side. They are accusing him of molesting one of the maids last night."

"We are aware of that," Letty said with mild scorn. "This is not the first time they've tried it."

Maggie was baffled. "You don't seem alarmed."

"There would be little point in being alarmed."

She stared at the English girl in disbelief. "I know that he thinks a great deal of you. Aren't you frightened for him at all?"

This time there was warmth in Letty's smile. "I have great confidence in Barnabas."

"You must have, or else you've little idea of the dreadful things being whispered about all of you."

She nodded. "I know the stories. Mrs. Judd is a witch and

I'm no better. And Barnabas is a vampire. Do you believe we are such a bad lot?"

"Of course not."

"Then that's all that matters," Letty said. "Barnabas will be happy when I inform him of your strong belief in him."

"I'm very confused," Maggie went on. "I need to talk to him, ask his advice. A lot has happened since I saw him last night."

"I understand how you feel," Letty said sympathetically. "And I will ask him to stop by Collinwood and discuss your problems with you tonight."

"Not before?"

"No. He is working. He would not thank me for interrupting him."

Maggie sighed. "Then it will have to be tonight but I'd rather he didn't come to the house."

"Where then?"

She thought a moment. "I'll go over to Widows' Hill at dusk. Ask him to meet me there."

"He'll be there. Barnabas has taken a great liking for you."

"And I'm fond of him," she admitted shyly.

Letty smiled again. "That's not too difficult for any of us. You're the girl who fell when you were out riding, aren't you?"

"Yes. And I'm still struggling to regain my memory."

"How distressing," Letty said. "I hope you make a quick recovery."

"In the meanwhile, I'm more dependent on Barnabas than I would otherwise be," Maggie explained.

"I understand." They began walking back towards the old house together.

Maggie felt the girl was sincere and her friend. She said, "Barnabas warned me that things were not what they seemed at Collinwood. And each hour I remain there I'm more convinced that he is right."

"Barnabas is a very wise man."

"I'm frightened," Maggie confessed. "I'd leave at once if I had my memory back."

"I think you'll be safe enough. At least for a short time."

"That is what Barnabas told me. Have you known him long?"

Letty smiled faintly. "It seems a lifetime. Actually, my grandmother and I have been his companions for several years."

"Asa Collins has asked him to leave here," she said. "When you do, where will you go?"

"That depends on Barnabas. He is a fanatic for travel. Already we have visited most of the chief cities of the world. He is a restless soul, not ever ready to settle down anywhere. I believe he has been most happy here."

"It is too bad he hasn't been given a kinder reception."

"We are used to cold treatment," Letty assured her. They had reached the door of the old house. "I will say goodbye now."

"We must meet again."

The blonde nodded. "I'm sure we will. And I'll give your message to Barnabas. He'll be waiting for you at dusk at Widows' Hill."

"I'll find some excuse to go out and meet him."

The blonde knocked on the door and a moment later her grandmother let her in. Letty waved to Maggie as she went inside. Maggie waved back and then proceeded on to Collinwood. Even though she hadn't managed to see Barnabas she felt somewhat better. Letty had a friendly, wholesome quality about her that was notably lacking in most of the people in the big mansion.

As she strolled slowly towards the grim house overlooking the ocean she wondered if Letty might be in love with Barnabas. Maggie felt a tiny twinge of jealousy; she had begun to feel a romantic attachment for him herself. Indeed, if Barnabas should ask her to run off and elope with him now she might readily accept the offer.

Even with her memory still impaired. She thought that much of him. And the lovely Letty had shown in every word that she doted on Barnabas; she was clearly as much in his confidence as anyone. Barnabas was lucky to have someone so practical to take charge of his living arrangements. The old woman was clearly too feeble to be anything more than a domestic. It would be Letty who managed things for him.

It annoyed Maggie to consider the dreadful things that were being said about the three occupants of the old house. No one who had met Letty could possibly think her a witch or in league with the Devil. She was a charming, strong-minded young woman and nothing more.

Fearful that the doleful line of consumptives might still be waiting, she decided to go around the other side of the house. This detour resulted in her coming upon old Asa Collins and Constable Withers in a serious conversation near the rose gardens. Seeing her they doffed their hats and bowed respectfully.

Asa Collins cleared his throat and in a gruff voice informed her, "The constable and I were reviewing the scene of last night's attack. I assume news of it has reached your ears?"

"I have heard about it," she said quietly.

Asa Collins nodded towards his companion. "Have you met Constable Withers?"

"No."

The constable bowed again, a smile on his broad face. "A pleasure to meet such a pretty young lady."

"Her name is Margaret Evans," Asa said gruffly, as if he didn't approve of the constable's comment. "She is a friend of Valeria's."

"Indeed," Constable Withers said with interest. "Did you hear or see anything last night?"

Remembering what she'd told Valeria and desiring to keep her story consistent, she said, "I heard a girl scream. And later I looked out the window and saw a huge bat."

The constable raised his eyebrows. "A bat, indeed. That fits in with the gardener's story." He looked at her keenly. "And did you see anything else?"

"No."

Asa Collins scowled at her. "You know Barnabas Collins, don't you?"

"I do," she said in a small voice.

"Valeria seems positive he was involved in the melee last night. You would have recognized him if you'd seen him, wouldn't you?"

"I would have."

"But you saw no one?" Withers asked her.

"No one."

"It might be well to keep your eyes open, Miss Evans," the constable said. "Something of this nature may happen again and we're sorely in need of information."

"I'll remember," she promised, anxious to be on her way. She turned to Asa Collins. "I'm going to the house. I chose this path to avoid passing by the patients waiting to enter the clinic."

He snorted angrily. "And wise you were. A veritable band of ragamuffins and malcontents if I am any judge. Were it not for Giles I'd have them horsewhipped off the grounds."

Maggie hastily excused herself and moved on. There was no one around when she entered the cool of the entrance hall and went upstairs to her own room. She had only been there a few minutes when there was a knock on her door and Valeria came in.

Valeria seemed in a vastly different mood from when she'd last seen her. Coming slowly across the room she smiled gently and declared, "You must hate me for the way I behaved in the conservatory."

She was surprised that her friend should bring this matter up again. Much better to have let it drop. "I'd almost forgotten about it."

"I'm glad," Valeria said impulsively. "I've been worried ever since. I said a lot of things I didn't mean."

"We all do that at times," Maggie said easily. But she was on her guard; she no longer quite trusted the other girl. She had a feeling there must be a reason for Valeria's sudden change of heart.

"I'm afraid the many tragedies here have left me overwrought," Valeria said. "And then Aunt Polly is an additional burden. I try to respect her since she is Giles' aunt. And while I'm living at Collinwood I represent Olive's family in the house. But that old woman is quite mad."

"Eccentric, perhaps. But would you say mad?"

"I would." Valeria looked at her very directly. "I glanced out the window and saw you two talking in the garden. Don't pay any attention to what she tells you."

"I'll remember that."

Now she knew what Valeria was up to. Fearful that the old woman had babbled something she shouldn't have, Valeria was trying to discredit anything Giles' aunt might have volunteered.

Valeria smiled sweetly. "You'll save yourself a great deal of annoyance if you do. Aunt Polly has some very strange delusions."

"That is common with the elderly," Maggie said with equal sweetness.

"I suppose so." Valeria crossed to the nearest window and looked out. "This room has an ideal view, hasn't it? I didn't realize it before."

"I like it."

Valeria turned to her again. "I had a dreadful headache this morning. That is why I behaved so badly. I've not been feeling well lately. Do you think it shows?"

Maggie, a little surprised, studied Valeria a moment. "I would say you're the picture of health."

"Thank you. You have no idea how happy that makes me. I suppose it is wrong but I'm terribly vain about my appearance."

"I see nothing wrong in pride of beauty."

"I'm glad you feel that way. I have guilty moments when I fear it may be sinful. But beauty is a gift and I think it would be wrong not to place a high value on it."

"Of course," Maggie said, not sure what the other girl was getting at.

"That was the great ordeal poor Olive suffered, the loss of her looks. It was harder on her than anything else. Her physical weakness was secondary; she was haunted by the way the disease ravaged her beauty. In the end she would allow no one but Giles to see her."

"So I've heard."

Valeria's lovely face had shadowed. "And she had always

been known as the true beauty of the family. Beside her I was the plain sister."

"Then she must have had unusual looks."

"She did." Valeria sounded preoccupied, as if her mind had wandered off into the past. "And yet when the disease hit, the change in her was noticeable almost at once."

"Giles was unable to do anything for her?"

Valeria shook her head. "No. He consulted the finest specialists. But they were all baffled by her condition. He was very frustrated. And it was only after that, following Olive's death, he established his clinic for consumptives."

"I see." Maggie recalled the gaunt man who had dragged his daughter away. He had implied that Giles was using the ill for his experiments, rather than attempting to cure them. Even though she no longer quite trusted Valeria and the young doctor, she did not think this was a fair accusation.

"Giles' father keeps threatening to make him close the clinic," Valeria went on. "But so far he has been able to carry on."

"Has he managed many cures?"

"That is hard to say. At least he is seeing that the unfortunate victims of the disease in this area are being given some sort of treatment. And he is trying to develop a vaccine to cure consumption."

"He must be dedicated to spend such long hours down there in the clinic."

"He is," the other girl assured her. "I think you should be happy that he is so fond of you."

Maggie felt her cheeks burn. "I haven't given it much thought."

"You should. He is a fine man. My sister and Giles had a perfect marriage. And from the moment I brought you here from Boston he has had eyes for no one else."

She felt she must be frank. "I'm not at all sure how I feel about him."

Valeria patted her arm. "Give romance a chance. Spend more time in his company. You'll not regret it."

"My feelings for him are quite negative."

"That is probably chiefly due to your fall," Valeria pointed out. "When you recover your memory, things will fall into a different perspective. You'll appreciate Giles for the man he is."

"You feel so strongly about him, yet you don't consider him as a husband?"

Valeria smiled sadly. "I would, if he hadn't been married to my sister. I'd never feel sure of his love. I'd always fear he was still in love with Olive and I was merely filling her role with him."

"I think I understand. But you could be very wrong."

"I daren't risk it," the other girl said with a sigh. "So he is yours, if you want him. And you would be foolish to ignore his love in favor of the attentions of someone like Barnabas."

At the mention of his name Maggie blushed. "I like Barnabas but I have never considered him seriously in a romantic way." This wasn't quite the truth but it was close —she had never believed that he could be interested in her.

Valeria's attractive face had gone hard again. "Surely you realize he is a person of loose morals. And he is involved with that blonde baggage who travels everywhere with him."

Maggie felt she should defend Barnabas. "I don't think he is that kind of person."

"You'll find out. He may not be a vampire, as the local people say, but I warrant you he has a taste for the village girls just the same."

Apparently pleased with this parting shot, Valeria left. Maggie found herself further confused. Her supposed friend had come to the room for a definite purpose: to discredit anything Aunt Polly had said and also put in a good word for Giles.

Artful as Valeria had been, she'd not done much more than make Maggie suspect her motives and increase her annoyance at the continued campaign against Barnabas. Besides, Maggie liked Letty. Even if the two were in love, no one had a right to condemn them. It was their business alone.

The rest of the day passed uneventfully. After dinner Giles sought her out in the rear parlor where she was sitting with Aunt Polly and suggested that he take her down to visit his laboratory.

"You have never visited my clinic in the cellar," he reminded her with a smile on his sensitive face.

"You've had a very busy day down there. Perhaps another time would be better."

"No," he insisted. "I'd like to show it to you tonight." She hesitated. Aunt Polly seemed to have slipped off into a doze. Anxious to escape the house and keep her rendezvous with Barnabas, Maggie was worried that the young doctor's invitation might interfere with her plans. On the other hand it would probably be better to keep him in good humor.

So she agreed, saying, "I would enjoy seeing the clinic. Afterward I'm going upstairs to my room. I'm still feeling the aftereffects of my accident."

His blue eyes were fixed on her. "Naturally. Well, come along."

Careful not to wake Aunt Polly, they left the room. Giles led the way down the hall and took a candle from a table and lighted it before he opened the door to the cellar steps.

He turned to her. "Watch the cellar steps," he warned. "They are uneven and worn from age."

She followed him down, lifting her skirt a trifle so as not to catch it in her heels. The floor of the cavern-like cellar was earthen and the place smelled of mold and dampness. All around them were storage areas and she began to wonder where his laboratory was.

"This way," he told her, turning to see that she was still close behind him. When they had walked a short distance further he opened a door. "Here we are," he said, and stood back for her to enter.

Maggie hesitantly stepped in, at once amazed at the contrast to the rest of the dank cellar. Even though the room was deeply shadowed she could see that its walls were paneled in fine wood and it had a shining hardwood floor. It contained a desk and chairs along with a great deal of complicated-looking tubes and equipment which she did not understand. In the far comer a blue flame burned under a glass container which bubbled and gurgled.

"Well, what do you think of it?" Giles asked with a touch of pride in his tone.

"Impressive," she told him, still taking in the surroundings. Just behind her there was an examining or operating table. And she noted that leather straps hung from its sides, obviously to be used to strap the patient down. It caused a tiny chill to ripple through her for she recalled hearing of the unbearable pain of tortured souls undergoing operations.

Giles had put down the candle and began to explain something about the room. His sensitive pale face took on a look of great animation as he told her of his experiments. Maggie was puzzled by his total neglect to bother mentioning the infectious nature of consumption.

She said, "Isn't the disease inclined to spread rapidly through entire households?"

"That happens," he said without interest. "My main occupation is with the blood and the changes that take place."

"I have heard that guarding people from the germ is all-important. When there is a parent or one child touched by consumption it is best to separate them from the rest of the family, isn't it?"

"That is a school of thought," Giles said impatiently. He moved quickly to the vessel over the flame with its bubbling liquid content. "This represents my effort to produce the ideal blood vaccine."

Making another try, she said, "I believe the germ of the

disease is common to animals, as well—that one can contact it through the contaminated milk of cows, for instance. Have you had any such cases?"

Giles turned to her with a fanatical gleam in his blue eyes. It was as if he'd not heard her. "The secret rests in the blood. Once I have conquered that, the other steps will be easy. The vaccine will assist in making the blood pure. A complete transference is what is required."

She stared at him in amazement. He had become so obsessed with this search for a cure-all vaccine that he might be considered unbalanced, on at least this one subject. The grim hours he had spent in this underground place had done something to him.

"I can understand your desire to perfect a vaccine. But in the meantime, what are you doing for these poor people?"

"I have given them the benefits of my experiments," he told her. "At various stages of the vaccine's development I have allowed them the advantage of it."

Her eyes widened. "You have injected them with the vaccine before perfecting it?"

His eyes still showed that unnatural glitter. "Why not? Many of them are within weeks of dying. They cannot afford to wait. A little help is better than none."

"But it may have no value at all."

"Not true!" he snapped. Turning his back on her, he busied himself at the counter where the liquid boiled under the alcohol flame.

She was astounded and fearful. Barnabas had told her that things in the old mansion were not all what they seemed. She was sure of it now. Had the death of Olive Collins caused Giles to lose his mind? What was he engaged in, under the pretense of attempting to cure consumptives?

Swallowing hard, she realized that he shouldn't be antagonized if he were insane on this subject. Quietly, she said, "I'm sorry. I didn't mean to say that. I suspect I was carried away by the excitement of what you are doing here."

He turned to her with a gloating look. "My hours here will make me famous one day."

"I trust that may be true," she said gravely.

He glanced at the bubbling liquid again. "I need to add more of a certain type of salts to this brew. I keep many of my supplies stored in the main area of the cellar. If you will excuse me for a moment." He bowed and quickly exited through the room's single door.

Maggie stood there uncertainly. She didn't like being

left alone; she wanted to get away from the room and the young doctor's company. By now, Barnabas would be at Widows' Hill waiting for her. Gazing fearfully around her in the shadowed atmosphere she wondered what sort of things went on in this room during the so-called clinic hours? What horror was being perpetrated here in the name of medicine? With a tiny shudder she moved away from the counter where the boiling liquid gurgled and stood by the other wall. For the first time she realized that this one wall was draped from ceiling to floor its full width. It suggested that the drapes might be concealing another room, perhaps a dressing room for the patients. Finding a parting in the drapes, she pulled them back to peer into the darkness beyond. And she gave a frightened scream! Standing there in the shadows was the phantom in pink!

CHAPTER 6

The withered face of the creature in pink showed the same expression of sheer hatred as before. Maggie gazed frozen at the phantom for a few seconds before letting the drape drop back in place. Then she ran across the laboratory to the door, nearly colliding with Giles, who had returned with a small cotton bag in his hand.

The young doctor showed astonishment. "What is wrong?"

She was on the edge of hysteria. Pointing to the drapes, she cried, "Back there! I saw it again! The phantom!"

He frowned at her. "You must be mistaken!"

"No!" she insisted. "I pulled back one of the drapes and she was standing there glaring at me. Look for yourself!"

"I will." He walked deliberately over to the drapes.

Maggie held her breath. He pulled the drape aside; there was no longer any sign of the ghost in pink. Nothing but a shadowed, empty anteroom.

"She was there! I saw her!"

Giles Collins allowed the drape to close again and turned to confront her with a strange expression. "You allowed your nerves to run away with your good sense," he suggested. "You imagined you saw someone there."

"But I did!"

He shook his head. "There is no exit from there except

through this room. It's quite impossible that you should have seen anyone."

She gave him a meaningful look. "Not even a ghost?"

His too-bright eyes burned into hers. "This is not the first time you've spoken to me of this phantom. And on neither occasion have I been able to see her."

Maggie felt drowned in shame and fear. She wondered if she was going to faint. There was a strange, sour odor in the room that added to her discomfort; it seemed to come from the boiling liquid over the alcohol flame. Why was Giles Collins so determined not to believe her?

The liquid in the glass container gurgled to break the silence that had come between her and the blond young man. Again she felt she could see the glint of madness in his eyes and she only could think of getting out of that dimly lighted room and away from him. "I must go back upstairs."

He studied her gravely. "Not for a moment," he said, moving so that he was between her and the door.

She gazed up into his pale, cold face with mounting fear. Her eyes wandered to the door only a few feet away from where they stood. But it might as well have been miles distant, with him blocking her way. "Please let me go."

"There's nothing to be afraid of."

"It's not that," she argued. "I'm feeling ill."

"I know how you are feeling," he said in an even tone, his eyes never leaving hers. "And I'm concerned about your health. To be brutally plain I'm upset about your mental condition. I fear the injury may have done you more harm than we at first guessed."

New panic seized her. "No!" she protested. "This has nothing to do with my fall."

"I think it does," he said coldly. "And I shall observe with interest whether the mania from which you suffer grows worse."

"I am not a lunatic."

"Your memory is gone and you admit to severe headaches."

"That's different!"

"Not necessarily," he said, his words bearing down on her hard. "It may be all part of the same parcel. Now you are seeing things and telling wild stories."

"What I said was true!"

His manner changed and he assumed a pose of hurt feelings and a hint of sadness. "You even seem to have developed hostile attitudes towards me."

Maggie looked at him hopelessly. "You're putting words in my mouth and assigning me thoughts that aren't mine."

"I want to help you."

"I'll be alright," she said. "Let us drop the matter."

"As a doctor I have a duty towards you," Giles maintained. "Unless you get over having these hallucinations, I must consider further treatment for you."

Maggie pictured the ragged unfortunates in his waiting line and thought of what he might be doing to them. She had no wish to become another of his experimental subjects, to find herself completely in his hands.

Quietly, she said, "Of course you're right. I must have imagined the phantom. Please allow me to go."

A sardonic expression crossed his good-looking face. "I'll be generous," he said. "But if I should hear one more word about your seeing the phantom, expect to be given a course of treatment."

"I understand," she said, too hastily.

"I have to stay here and add some of this to my vaccine," he said, holding up the small bag. "I'll see you as far as the steps and you can manage the rest of the way on your own."

"Of course!"

He had his hand on the doorknob but still he hesitated. "Remember, I'll expect you to make no mention of a phantom to Valeria or any of the others upstairs."

"I won't." She was ready to say anything so long as she was allowed to leave.

"We'll discuss this more another time."

He opened the door and guided her back through the blackness of the main cellar. This time he carried no candle. He'd left the door of the laboratory open to offer them a faint glow of illumination from in there. But the amount of light they got from this was hopeless. She stumbled once and he had to quickly catch her in his arms to prevent her from falling.

When they reached the foot of the steep stone steps, he said, "Keep one hand against the wall to guide you. It's straight up and the door up there opens out into the hallway."

"Thank you."

"I hope you haven't misunderstood my concern for your health," he said in a gentler tone. "I'm thinking of your interest."

"I'll remember that."

"Have a good night's rest, Margaret," he told her. "And try to dismiss those nightmare visions from your mind." He took her in his arms for a moment and touched his lips briefly to hers.

Then she was mounting the stairs, faltering in the darkness, terrified she might stumble again and this time suffer a bad fall. At last her groping hand found the door and she opened it to step into the familiar and welcome atmosphere of the ground floor hallway.

She closed the door behind her, wishing that this would also shut the unpleasantness she'd encountered below from her life. But she knew that it wouldn't. And she was more convinced than before that Giles Collins had a touch of madness and his experiments down there were diabolical.

Darkness had settled. Barnabas Collins would be waiting at Widows' Hill for her. It would be cool on that cliff by the ocean; she would need a cloak. And to get one she'd have to journey up to her room and then find her way out of the old mansion without being seen. It was going to be a test of nerves for her.

The entrance hall was deserted. From the front parlor she could hear the gruff voice of old Asa Collins in subdued conversation with Aunt Polly. She went up the broad stairway swiftly, careful to make no sound.

She was almost up to her own landing when Valeria appeared. The dark girl came down the stairs to meet her half-way. Valeria said, "I saw you go with Giles. I imagine he was showing you his laboratory."

"He was."

"Did you find it interesting?" Valeria was studying her closely.

"Very. But I had to ask him to let me leave. I have a headache."

Valeria raised her eyebrows. "Another one?"

"They seem to come on at nights," Maggie improvised desperately.

"That's too bad. I hope it passes soon."

"So do I," she said. And then exchanging goodnights with Valeria she hurried on up to her room.

She put on a navy blue cloak and waited in her room until she felt reasonably sure Valeria would be out of the way. Then she crept down the stairs as gently as she'd ascended them. No one appeared on the stairways or in the hall. And she was able to slip out the front door unobserved.

Taking a deep breath of the bracing night air, she felt better at once. Just being out in the open was a tonic. Something in the very atmosphere of the sinister old mansion intimidated her and made her doubly frightened. She set out across the lawn in the direction of the cliffs.

This night was as dark as last night had been bright with moonlight. There were not even any stars. Judging by the black clouds she guessed that a storm was on its way. From the time of her accident there had been only sunny, warm days at Collinwood. And her memory did not extend beyond her fall. A rainstorm would break the pattern. Maybe her memory would return with it.

She held her cloak tightly around her, grateful the night was so black. It would serve to conceal her. This meeting with Barnabas Collins must be a secret. If Giles or Valeria caught them together again they might be moved to increase their efforts to cause Barnabas further trouble.

Only now was she beginning to get a true picture of what was going on at the brooding old house. And she liked no part of it. If Giles Collins was not mad he was evil. And Valeria was surely in league with him in those infamous experiments of his.

Perhaps Asa Collins was the most dependable of all those gathered under the roof of the mansion. The old man might be gruff and unbending, but he did appear to be a person of principle. And he had openly expressed his displeasure with his doctor son, although he seemed to get along well enough with Valeria.

Maggie had reached the path that followed the edge of the cliffs now. She hurried along in the darkness. The only touch of light to break the enveloping gloom was the pinpoint of the Collinsport lighthouse beam as it sent out its warning to passing ships. The sound of the waves on the shore far below was for her a mournful dirge.

She began to worry that she had come too late, that Barnabas had been there and gone. Her heart began to pound with fear at the thought. What would she do? And how safe would she be in this isolated place alone? Memory of the grim withered face of the pink phantom came to her vividly.

She'd reached the high point of the cliffs known as Widows' Hill. Halting, she held the cloak tightly around her and peered into the black night. There was no sign of Barnabas. She didn't know what to do. She was unwilling to return to the mansion without seeing him and she was also afraid to make the return journey alone. She'd exhausted all her courage in this frantic effort to meet him. The expectation of talking to him had given her the impetus to make the excursion into the night. But now she felt only despair.

The minutes passed and she still stood there. Finally, suddenly, she saw a movement in the shadows to the right of her.

Hopefully she called out, "Barnabas?"

"Yes." The reply came in his familiar voice. And he quickly emerged from the darkness to join her.

"I was positive I'd missed you," she confessed nervously. "I was late getting away."

He nodded. "I was here before. But I guessed you might have been detained. So I came back."

"I'm glad," she said with relief. She could only see the outline of his profile in the darkness; the expression on his handsome face was lost to her. "It's been a horrid day."

"You sound very upset."

"I am."

"I decided that when I heard you had come to the old house asking for me today," Barnabas Collins said in mild reproof. "I made a definite request that you would not do anything like that."

She bowed her head contritely. "I'm sorry."

"It was fortunate that you met Letty and she was able to give me your message later."

"I meant no harm."

"But I explained I wasn't to be disturbed in the daytime."

Maggie looked up at him. "I don't understand that."

He shrugged. "Must you understand everything? Aren't you willing to show some faith in me?"

"I suppose so," she said reluctantly. "But it seems very odd that you never show yourself in daylight. I can realize why the villagers would seize on the idea you are a vampire."

"What do you know of vampires?" There was an edge in the voice of the man standing there in the darkness with her. She could almost feel his tension grow.

She tried to sound casual. "Not very much, I'm afraid. But enough to know they have to avoid the daylight and that they survive by attacking the living and feasting on their blood."

"Do you believe in such things?"

"I suppose not. But many people are superstitious enough to," she pointed out. "That is why I think you are doing yourself needless harm by playing the recluse as you do."

"Perhaps you are right." He sounded relaxed again.

"I'm sure of it. With these weird stories circulating about you and the old woman and Letty, you should avoid any appearance of evil. Giles and Valeria will use anything they can against you."

"What have you discovered about those two to make you so concerned?"

"I'm positive now that your warning was well timed. I don't trust either of them."

"That is wise," Barnabas said dryly.

"For some reason they both hate and fear you. The constable was at the house today and Valeria accused you of attacking a maid on the grounds last night."

"Indeed?"

She hesitated. "I heard the girl scream. And I saw you crossing the lawn in the moonlight afterward. But I didn't tell them I saw you."

"Oh? Why?" Barnabas asked suavely.

"Because I know it must have been a coincidence. I'm sure you're not capable of making such an attack. It is not your nature."

"Thank you," he said warmly. "I doubt if I warrant your high opinion of me, but I assure you I'm most grateful for it."

"Something horrible is going on at Collinwood," she said urgently. "I found that out today. That clinic Giles is operating isn't really for the benefit of those poor sick creatures who come to him for treatment. It's a ruse he's using to get victims for his mad experiments."

"I'm afraid that's very likely."

"Until today I didn't dream anyone could be capable of such a wicked, cruel thing," she said. "I'm ready to believe that Giles Collins is mad. The tragic fate of his wife drove him out of his mind."

"It's possible," Barnabas agreed. "I hear he was deeply in love with Olive. And she was a beauty."

"That's why her death was so horrible. Her illness wasted away all her looks."

"That still doesn't give him the right to torture those unfortunates and lead them to believe he is going to help them."

"I know it. He must be stopped."

"That could be difficult."

"His father is against the clinic," she said. "If he became angry enough, he might make Giles close it."

"I wouldn't count on that," Barnabas warned her. "Giles is just as strong-willed as his father."

"And Valeria is encouraging him in whatever is going on."

"She probably has a reason," he suggested calmly. "She must know the entire story of his experiments and the reason for them. Could it be that he used his late wife as a guinea pig for some of his vaccines and so caused her illness and death?"

Maggie gasped. "I hadn't thought of that. It could have been that way."

"Valeria always stood in the shadow of her sister, I understand," Barnabas went on. "Perhaps it gave her a certain satisfaction to watch as Olive was robbed of her looks. The rivalry between sisters can often be a vicious thing."

"Valeria might have encouraged him to try the vaccine on his wife, hoping that it would destroy her." She paused. "But if that is true, wouldn't Giles hate her for it? And he seems to be very friendly with her."

"There could be reasons for that we don't understand. But the fact remains Olive Collins died under mysterious circumstances and was buried in the night."

She looked up at him earnestly. "Barnabas, what are we going to do? I'm afraid to remain there any longer. And yet I'm afraid to leave with my memory a blank. And only tonight he hinted that he thought the fall might have upset my mind."

"Count on him to suggest others as mad as himself."

"I saw that phantom in pink again," she explained. "That's how it came about. And when it had vanished by the time he arrived, he chose to suggest I'd imagined it."

"That would be convenient."

"And I know I didn't," she protested. "I've seen her more than that. The first time it was in my room on the night after my accident."

"I remember your telling me about it."

"Collinwood is haunted," she exclaimed, glancing back through the darkness in the direction of the old house.

"And that woman in pink has come to me as a warning. It has to be!"

"And yet you cannot leave until you are well." "Maybe I should go anyway," she worried. "It would be different if you were in the house."

"I will give you all the protection I can."

"It might not be enough."

"I think if you persevere you will learn all their guilty secrets," he said. "And it could be you will be the instrument to destroy the evil that has come to Collinwood." She stared at him in the shadows, trying to make out the expression on his handsome face. But she couldn't. She said, "Why do you say that? You talk as if you knew what was going on."

"I can only guess," he said. "And there is little I can do alone. But with you in the house there is a real chance of defeating them."

She was slow in answering, her face drawn with fear as she listened to the pounding of the waves at the bottom of the cliff. "I'm terrified," she confessed.

"That is natural."

"You're asking me to be a decoy?"

"You could call it that."

"I feel so helpless," she protested. "What might happen to me if they somehow eliminate you? And you know that is what they're trying to do."

"Because they fear me. They are sure I know their secret."

"How long do you think it might take to settle with them?"

"Not long," he said. "I mean to leave here soon. I'd want to see it over before I go."

"Where will you be going?"

"I haven't decided. I'm a wanderer, you know."

"And they'll be going with you, of course. I mean Mrs. Judd and Letty."

"Yes."

"Letty is very beautiful."

"It would be hard not to notice that," Barnabas admitted readily. "And she is as wise as she is lovely. She will help us in this all she can."

"I'm not sure I want her help."

"Why not?" Barnabas sounded surprised.

She shrugged. "Maybe I'm jealous of her. She is the one you love, isn't she?"

"A man in my position has little time for romance," he said, returning to his aloof manner.

"You haven't denied it."

Barnabas took her by the arms and gazed at her intently. She could feel his eyes on her despite the darkness. "You must think of other things," he told her. "Your main concern should be correcting the evil at Collinwood." The concealing shadows gave her courage to say what was in her heart.

"That is not easy, Barnabas, when I find that I've fallen in love with you."

His hold on her arms tightened and he uttered a sound of despair. "I don't believe it."

"It's true," she told him quietly.

"I blame myself," he said bitterly. "I should not have been so friendly."

"You're not to blame, nor am I," she said. "It's happened. I realize you're in love with Letty and so it's just my misfortune. But I had to make you understand."

"I'm truly fond of you, Maggie," he said in a gentler tone. "Never doubt that." And he held her close and their lips met for a lasting kiss. In the thrill of that happiness Maggie barely noted the icy coldness of his lips. But later she would remember.

He let her go and said, "Now you must return to the house. I have things to attend to. And they must not guess you came here to meet me."

"When will I see you again?"

"Soon," he said. "I may call by Collinwood tomorrow night. If I do I'll somehow manage a few minutes alone with you. If not tomorrow night, soon after."

"And what can I do in the meantime?"

"Behave as if you weren't in the least aware that anything is wrong there," he advised her. "And keep your eyes and ears open."

"I'm sure they're suspicious of me now."

"But they can't be sure," he said. "Come. I'll see you back a good part of the way."

They were no more than twenty yards from the main entrance to the mansion when he halted and said a final goodnight. She hurried the rest of the way, consoled by the knowledge that he was still there watching over her. The door was not bolted, so she quietly let herself in.

There was no lamp in the entrance hall and all was silence. She stood just inside the door staring up the broad stairway. A dim light showed down from above. She was about to start up the stairs when she heard the sound of footsteps from the rear of the lower hallway. Quickly she withdrew into the shadows of the parlor entrance, hoping she wouldn't be discovered.

It was a girl, one of the maids who had brought her breakfast. The girl also had the air of being worried that someone might see her. She hesitated in the front hall to glance apprehensively up the stairs. In the faint light Maggie could see that the girl still wore a tiny apron over her dress. Then the maid moved on and opened the front door carefully and left the house.

Maggie was astonished. With a frown on her pretty face she went to a nearby window to stare out into the darkness and follow the girl's progress across the lawn. The maid walked directly to the spot where Barnabas had been standing. And she had no doubt that the two were even now strolling off into the night together.

The incident gave her a bad jolt. It was plain that at least part of the gossip about Barnabas being a ladies' man was true. Giles Collins had not been too far from the facts, nor had Valeria. Barnabas had been anxious to get her back to the house at once because he'd known the maid would soon be out to meet him. Should she hate him for this? Was it fair to judge him on this evidence? She couldn't decide. But what she'd seen had made her unhappy.

Bewildered and weary, she started up the steps. As she reached the second landing and walked down the hallway to her own room she had the eerie feeling that she was being watched; that somewhere close, unseen eyes were following her. She fought back her rising panic and increased her pace. As she came to her own door mocking feminine laughter rang out. And behind her in the darkness the door of one of the other rooms closed.

CHAPTER 7

The following morning Maggie awoke to the pelt of raindrops on her windows. The day was starting out gray and wet. She lay there for long minutes listening to the rain and thinking of the events of the previous day and night. And she couldn't help wincing as she recalled the girl who had crept out in the night to meet Barnabas.

It was more than mere jealousy with her. The relationship between the girl and Barnabas could offer great danger for him. She was positive that he was not taking the vicious campaign Valeria and Giles were waging against him seriously enough. A single misstep on his part and he would know the full weight of their intolerance.

She raised herself on an elbow and stared at the rain streaking down the window pane. The somber day suited her mood. Why had she consented to stay on at this horrible, bewildering place? The midnight tryst between Barnabas and the servant girl had shaken her faith in his judgment.

She got out of bed and slipped into a robe, then went over to the dresser and began to brush her long dark hair. Another thing that troubled her was the feeling that she was being continually spied upon and jeered at by the phantom in pink. Why didn't anyone else ever see it?

She was sure the malicious laugh she'd heard in the dark hallway last night had come from the ghostly crone in the pink cowl and flowing robe. But not even the sound of the closing door had enabled her to guess exactly where the mocking laugh had originated.

For one thing, she'd been too terrified to search the area afterward. And she was reasonably sure she wouldn't have discovered anything if she had. Yet she somehow felt that all the evil in Collinwood was personified by the creature in pink with the withered hag's face.

Her reverie was interrupted by a mild knock on her door. It would be one of the servants with her breakfast tray. She paused in the grooming of her hair to turn and say, "Yes. Come in."

The young maid who entered smiled hesitantly. "A nasty morning, miss." She moved quickly across the room to place the tray on a small table near the window.

"It is," Maggie agreed in a vague voice, for she had been taken by surprise. This was the same girl she'd seen going out to meet Barnabas last night. At least no harm had come to her. She said, "I think you've brought me breakfast before, but I don't remember your name."

The girl looked up from arranging the tray and smiled. She had a pert oval face. "Mabel. Yes, I have brought your breakfast several times."

"I was sure of that, Mabel," she said, still appraising the girl.

Mabel crimsoned under her scrutiny. "Is there anything else, miss?"

"No, not now."

"Very well, miss," the maid said, bowing her head slightly again before she went on out and closed the door after her.

Maggie stood there frowning to herself. She had purposely been careful to study the girl's graceful throat. And the red mark had been there. It had been too definitely outlined to miss. So this was the weird spot left on the throats of the other girls who had claimed to have been attacked. But Mabel was making no such claim. What did it mean?

She sat down to breakfast but found her appetite had deserted her. She spent more time morosely staring out at the heavy rain and sipping coffee than in eating any of the hearty fare on the silver tray. Her eyes fixed gloomily on the tall pines glistening with dripping rain as she debated whether the whispers concerning Barnabas might be true or not.

She had been emphatic in denying Valeria's assertion that he was a vampire and that the two women in the old house with him were in some way linked to black magic; now she could only wonder. There was a sad, withdrawn air about Barnabas. Did it signify more than that he was a sensitive man? Could he be the monster the others claimed? One of the walking dead?

She racked her memory for things she had heard about such creatures. It seemed that someone had told her vampires had the unhealthy putty color of a corpse. And Barnabas did have sallow skin. What else was there? Coldness to the touch, dark hairs on the palms of the hands and unusually long, white teeth behind thick lips. All these details could be listed in a description of Barnabas!

It was a frightening realization. Other peculiarities of the vampires came to mind. Didn't they—like Barnabas— avoid daylight and walk the earth only from dusk to dawn? But she'd be as bad as the villagers if she indicted him for that alone. What other indications were important? Then she recalled that a vampire's reflection would not show in a mirror. Surely that could be a test.

Suddenly she was furious with herself. After all, Barnabas was her only friend, the one person she felt she could count on at the moment. How dare she even consider his being a vampire? It was too ridiculous. With a sigh she put down her empty coffee cup and took up her hairbrush. It was to finish with her hair and get dressed.

Normally she went straight downstairs and often on out to the garden. Today this was out of the question. As she was not anxious to encounter any of the others she made up her mind to explore the upstairs of the house. To the best of her knowledge she'd never done it before and it was an interesting old place. She might have been given a tour of the upper regions before she'd fallen and lost her memory but nothing of it remained with her.

It was still raining hard as she went out into the hallway and headed down the opposite corridor. It was narrow and shadowed even in daylight. She had never bothered going along this section of the hallway. But now the exploration held interest for her. From somewhere down here the nasty chuckle had come the previous night.

She'd reached the end of the corridor when she came upon something that made her halt and gasp. A section of the wall had been bricked off. And the lime between the bricks was fresh enough to suggest that it had been done only recently. The bricks rose from floor to ceiling and surely a door had been concealed behind them. But why?

"You find this odd?" a familiar voice asked.

Maggie wheeled around to see Aunt Polly standing there with a taunting smile. "Yes, it does seem unusual."

"That is where Olive died. The very room."

"Oh?" Maggie stared at the bricks again.

"Giles did it. After she died, he had the room bricked off from the rest of the house."

"I see," she said. "What was his idea in doing it?"

The old woman shrugged. "I expect his mind was twisted with grief. He hasn't been his old self since Olive's death. And she wasn't worth his mourning as he did, for all her pretty face!"

"Why do you say that?" Maggie asked, giving her a startled glance.

The old woman wore a gloating expression. "I knew her better than most. And I had to keep my place, as they say, when she was alive and the mistress of the house. But I can speak plainly now."

"You make it sound as if she wasn't the perfect person Giles claims."

"Far from it!" Aunt Polly snapped. "And for all his mealy-mouthed talk about her now, they fought often enough when she was alive. That Olive could be a vixen when she liked."

Maggie's eyes were wide with amazement. "I assumed they were a very happy couple."

"Far from it," the old woman repeated venomously. "Olive had a nasty temper and Giles wasn't one to let her have her own way. So die house was always uneasy."

"Perhaps he regrets the quarrels," she suggested. "That is why he has gone to such lengths in his grief and mourns her so now."

"It could be he blames himself for what happened to her."

"How do you mean? She had an incurable disease. That surely wasn't his fault."

"He'd already been spending long hours in the cellar working on some kind of mysterious vaccine. And I heard him persuading her to let him try it on her."

Maggie was suddenly aware that she might be about to hear something important.

"Did she agree?"

"I think so," the old woman said. "He was bribing her. Offering her a precious pearl necklace that had belonged to his mother. Asa always had kept it in his safe. But Giles promised to get it from him and give it to her as payment for her help in testing his vaccine."

Maggie was studying the old woman in the shadowed corridor, trying to decide how much to believe. It was hard to say. At times Aunt Polly appeared shrewd and competent; then again she gave the impression of having slipped into senility.

"Did you actually hear her agree to take the vaccine?"

"No."

"Then you can't be sure that she did."

Aunt Polly's rheumy eyes glittered triumphantly. "I'm pretty sure she did. Because a day or so later I saw her wearing the pearls."

Maggie was silenced for a moment by this. Had Giles wrecked his wife's beauty and brought about her premature death with his mad experiments? The rain beat against the window at the end of the corridor as a suitable background for her melancholy thoughts.

Finally she said, "The pearls were the ones he'd mentioned? You're sure of that?"

"I've seen them enough times to know. After Olive died, the pearls disappeared. I asked Giles about them and he pretended not to know what I was talking about."

"He may have been telling you the truth. You could have been confused about it all. Misunderstood the conversation between him and Olive as well."

"I don't think so," Aunt Polly said with assurance. "I watched as he made an old woman out of her in a few months. It was toward the end when Olive had shut herself in her room that Valeria came here."

"That must have been a comfort to Olive."

"Small comfort, when the two had always hated each other." Maggie frowned. "No one told me that."

"I can tell you," Aunt Polly replied. "And I know. Olive didn't want that green-eyed hussy here. It was Giles who arranged for her to come."

"Even that is understandable," Maggie said. "He may have needed someone to help him through those difficult days. Valeria would know her sister better than most."

"That's the smooth talk they tried to make me swallow," Aunt Polly responded indignantly. "But I know Olive didn't want her."

Maggie sighed. "Well, she died and it's all over now."

Aunt Polly gave her a mocking smile. "Not quite."

"What do you mean?"

The old woman nodded at the brick wall. "I don't think it was grief that made Giles brick up her room. I say it was guilt. And I don't think the wall will save him. Her avenging spirit still dominates this house and she'll break through the wall to even accounts with Dr. Giles Collins before she rests in her grave."

"You're talking about ghosts again."

The rheumy eyes met hers. "You claim to have been visited by one."

"That's different."

"I know you've made Giles jumpy with your stories, but I believe them. And I say it's Olive you've seen."

Maggie was shocked. She said, "The figure I've seen is that of an old, old woman with a thin, wrinkled face."

"Olive was a hag with a withered face when Giles finished trying his devil's potion on her," Aunt Polly reminded her.

"I still can't connect any of it," Maggie protested. Aunt Polly's words had brought a number of wild thoughts to mind. Again she realized how little she knew of the truth about what had gone on in Collinwood and what was going on there now.

The stout woman eyed her malevolently. "Valeria brought you here to hush up any scandal. He knew that Asa didn't like his son having her in the house here with him so soon after Olive's death. So she went to Boston and found poor silly you!"

Maggie stared at her. "I don't remember the circumstances."

"Valeria tricked you into coming here for a holiday. And then Giles played his part by pretending to fall in love with you. He's even gotten Asa believing that. But I don't believe it."

"What do you believe?"

"He's in love with Valeria. And she with him! It began long before Olive took sick and died. They're using you as a pawn."

"You make it sound very unpleasant and cruel."

"That is what it is," Aunt Polly said firmly.

"I'm sorry," Maggie said. "I don't see this in the melodramatic light you do. I admit to being confused. But when I'm able to remember I'm certain everything will fall properly in place."

"Maybe your eyes will be opened and you'll find what I'm saying is true," Aunt Polly told her. "Your accident was pure luck for them. It has put you even more at their mercy. And I pity you when they haven't any further use for you."

Maggie felt fresh fear welling up in her. "Why are you telling me all this?"

The old woman curled her lip. "Not for love of you, you know that. But because I hate them. They want to see me sent away from here, have me rot away my last days in some fetid ward with the hopelessly insane. But they haven't managed it yet! I still have Asa on my side!" Aunt Polly's voice had risen and her lips were flecked with an overflow of saliva from her sudden surge of anger.

Maggie was startled and repulsed. "I don't think we should discuss it any more."

Aunt Polly had now recovered some composure. She smoothed her dress front with her brown, heavily-veined hands. "Perhaps you are right," she said in a milder tone. "When I think about these things I get carried away."

"I'm sure your fears are unfounded," Maggie told her, although privately she wondered.

"You depend too much on Barnabas," the old woman said abruptly.

She stared at her. "What has he to do with it?"

"Just what I said. You think he can save you. It is doubtful if he can save himself. He has remained at Collinwood too long this time."

"This time? I supposed it was his first visit."

Aunt Polly smiled mysteriously. "Did he tell you that?"

"I think he did."

"Better ask him again. And you can tell him from me that Giles knows his weakness and is working to make him take the blame for many things."

"What things?"

"Barnabas will understand." The old woman turned and walked off down the shadowed hallway.

Maggie watched her go with a feeling of fear and annoyance. Had she been listening to the truth about things at Collinwood or had the sight of the brick wall merely started Aunt Polly off on a wild string of fantasies? She gave the ominous-looking wall a final worried glance and then followed the old woman down the hallway. But by the time she reached the head of the stairs there was no sign of Aunt Polly.

She decided to return to her own room for a little. Once again she rebelled at the knowledge that she could not contact Barnabas until dusk had arrived. And as usual that thought brought her the familiar uneasiness that the stories about him might be true. Vampires slept in their coffins during the daylight hours.

With this grim doubt nagging in the back of her mind she opened the door to her own room and went in. At once she halted in surprise and stood staring at the unexpected intruder standing there facing her. It was none other than Barnabas' housekeeper, Mrs. Judd!

She gasped, "What are you doing here?"

The old woman had a shawl about her head and wore a black cloak. Her smile was toothless and knowing. "Miss Letty sent me."

"How did you manage to get in here?"

"No one ever notices me."

Maggie was further astonished. No wonder they called the old woman a witch. "What do you want?"

"Miss Letty said you were to come to the house."

"Now?"

"Yes."

Maggie hesitated. "But Barnabas doesn't like me going to the house during the day. He scolded me for my other visit there."

"When Miss Letty sends for anyone, it's wise for them to take note."

"It's something urgent then," Maggie said. She began to feel panicky. If Barnabas were truly in danger she surely wanted to know all about it. She couldn't refuse the summons.

"Miss Letty is waiting for you," the ancient crone murmured.

"Very well, I'll go."

"I'll tell her." Mrs. Judd sounded satisfied.

Maggie hurried over to the closet for her cloak. By the time she'd located it and turned to speak to Mrs. Judd there was no sign of her. She was alone in the room!

It gave her an eerie feeling, the way Mrs. Judd appeared and vanished soundlessly. Again Maggie was struck by the resemblance between Mrs. Judd and the phantom in pink. Could the housekeeper be posing as the ghost of Collinwood for some strange reason?

She realized there was no time for her to stand there debating questions which were unanswerable in any case. Slipping into the cloak and carefully adjusting its cowl over her head, she left her room and started downstairs. The hallways and stairs were especially dark on this somber, wet day. She reached the entrance hall before she encountered anyone. And then it was the beautiful Valeria who showed herself in the doorway of the living room.

"You're braving this awful rain?"

Maggie was embarrassed. "Yes. It's not cold. And I like to walk in the rain."

Valeria's eyebrows lifted. "I don't recall you ever mentioning this before."

"I must have."

"It's a downpour," Valeria said. "You'll soon have enough of it."

"I may not go far."

"Keep away from the cliff path," Valeria warned. "It can be very slippery on a day like this. And before you realized you could lose your footing and topple down on the rocks."

"I'll be careful," Maggie promised. She had serious doubts about the dark girl's apparent concern for her safety. Keeping in mind what Aunt Polly had said, she was more and more convinced Valeria was merely using her for a dupe.

As Maggie started towards the door Valeria moved into the hallway to intercept her. The dark girl's eyes met hers as she asked, "Was Aunt Polly boring you with more of her nonsensical talk a little while ago?"

She didn't know what to say. Judging by the suspicion on Valeria's pretty face, she must have been somewhere near enough to overhear them. To deny the conversation would only make things worse.

So she said, "We did meet upstairs. For the first time I'd come upon the brick wall Giles installed to shut off his wife's room. I was startled until she explained its significance to me."

"Indeed," Valeria said coldly. "I doubt her competence to do that."

Maggie forced a smile. "She rambled a little but she did try to be helpful." She hoped this would satisfy Valeria and allay her fears.

"I trust you didn't accept her version of things as true."

"You warned me about her."

"It was stupid of Giles to indulge in such a sentimental gesture in the first place," Valeria said with annoyance. "I tried to discourage him from the idea. But men can be stubborn when they like. It was his way of showing how much he cared for Olive. He shut off the room just as she left it."

"Aunt Polly told me that."

"And a lot more I'll wager," Valeria said. "I must instruct her not to keep annoying you."

"I don't mind."

Valeria smiled coldly. "That's generous of you, Maggie. But you are my guest and I do feel a responsibility towards you. Especially since your unfortunate accident."

"I appreciate that," Maggie said in a quiet voice. "But I have grown quite fond of Aunt Polly so you mustn't reprimand her on my behalf."

"You're extremely generous," Valeria said with a sour smile. "Don't remain out too long."

She promised that she wouldn't and then stepped out into the rain. As she slowly made her way across the lawn she sensed Valeria watching her from the parlor window. And she feared that she might be followed when she changed her direction to head for the old house. Valeria would have time to go down to the laboratory in the cellar and tell Giles of her excursion into the downpour.

Visions of the doctor pursuing her and taking her to task nagged at her. She was becoming more afraid of both Valeria and Giles. The things that Aunt Polly had told her were etched in her mind.

Reaching the shelter of several elms standing close together she took advantage of their refuge from the worst of the downpour to stare back at the grim mansion. There was no sign of anyone trailing her. She decided she would wait in the shadow of the trees for a little and then quickly proceed to the old house. This way she was reasonably sure of not being followed.

How different Collinwood appeared to her now! From a pleasant country house it had been transformed in her eyes into a dark place concealing madness and lust . . . and deadly danger. She shivered at the thought.

She had waited long enough. Now she would go keep the rendezvous with Letty. Barnabas must be in some sort of trouble or the girl wouldn't have sent for her. This was the unpleasant truth she had to face. With a final glance at the ominous outline of Collinwood she braved the rain again to hurry along the path past the outbuildings.

The rain had not eased at all. She bent her head against the storm, turning now and then to see if there was anyone behind her. She seemed to have eluded any pursuer. Reaching the old house, she found it even more bleak on this unpleasant day. The shutters were closed as always and it had the usual air of desertion.

She mounted the steps and knocked on the oaken door confident that Mrs. Judd must have announced she was coming. She had a forlorn hope that Barnabas might open the door himself, but when it finally did swing back to reveal the dark passage it was Letty who stood there, looking pale and concerned. "Thank you for coming so promptly."

"Mrs. Judd suggested your message was urgent."

Letty closed the door and they stood facing each other in the shadowed passage. "I did want to ask you a few questions before I talked with Barnabas."

"Where is he?"

"Downstairs," Letty said. "He has a room furnished down there. It spares him needless interruptions. Please come into the living room." The English girl led the way.

Maggie followed her, shocked by the dampness of the old house and the sad state of its disrepair. The wallpaper was sagging and actually peeling off the wall in several places. Everywhere there was dust and the floor was grimy with worn carpeting showing damp rot in spots.

Entering the living room, she gazed around in utter confusion. It was like a room in a house closed for years! Cobwebs hung from the ceiling and in the corners. The furniture was thick with dust and the chairs had shroudlike coverings. Even the lamp seemed not to have been used in ages. A heavy coating of dust covered its fancy shade.

Letty, noticing her amazement, said, "We do not come in here often. But then I did not invite you over to apologize for my bad housekeeping."

Maggie came to the point at once. "Is there some trouble?"

"There could be," Letty said, studying her. "You saw Barnabas last night, didn't you?"

"Yes."

"When you left him, did he by any chance meet someone else? A maid from Collinwood named Mabel?"

CHAPTER 8

Maggie couldn't conceal her surprise at the calm question. "I believe the girl did go out to meet him. I saw her leave the house when I came in."

"I thought so," Letty said with a strange expression on her attractive face.

"Her name is Mabel, as you said. She's a maid at Collinwood. In fact, I talked to her this morning. She brought me my breakfast."

Letty's face brightened. "I'm glad to hear that. I was worried about her."

Maggie stared at the English girl. "Did you think she might have come to some harm through Barnabas?" Immediately Letty became wary.

She said, "I was afraid something might have happened to her and Barnabas would be blamed. I've warned him against seeing her."

"Did he tell you about last night?"

"He was evasive. The situation here is becoming complicated. I think it would be well for you to leave before it is too late."

"Too late?" Her eyes widened. "But Barnabas has asked me to remain."

"I'm worried for him as well as you," Letty said. "In fact, it is his safety which concerns me most; you are welcome to take what risks you like. As long as Barnabas doesn't wind up paying the bill for them."

"I'd prefer to discuss this with him," she said. "Maybe then I can decide what I'd better do."

"Don't you have any confidence in my judgment at all?"

"I look to Barnabas for guidance," Maggie responded resolutely.

The blonde was standing behind one of the covered chairs, her hands gripping its back. She gave Maggie a glance of silent contempt before she said, "You don't even know the kind of man Barnabas Collins is!"

"I think I do."

Letty's eyes bored into her. "Why not admit the truth? You are in love with him, aren't you?"

She blushed angrily. "Even if I should be, is it any business of yours?"

"Yes. I think so. Mrs. Judd and I are with Barnabas to protect him. We were engaged for that purpose. And I would be negligent in my duties if I didn't act in his best interests and warn you that any romance between you and him is hopeless."

Maggie smiled bitterly. "I didn't need the warning. He has already admitted that. He as much as said that he was already in love with you."

This seemed to take the English girl by surprise. She waited a moment before saying, "Did he? And what are you hoping? That in time he will change his mind?"

She shrugged. "Perhaps."

"He won't."

"I'm prepared for that."

Letty eyed her coldly. "Are you also prepared to watch the man you claim to love be destroyed? And in part destroyed because of your presence here and his wish to help you?"

"It is I who have been asked to help him," she protested.

"I don't know how you've decided on that," Letty said. "But I will tell you that Valeria Norris and that young doctor are deliberately setting a trap for Barnabas. He is to be their scapegoat."

"Barnabas is a very competent and intelligent man. I'm sure he can outwit them."

"I wish I had your confidence." Letty sounded grim. "When you see him next you would be doing him a favor if you urged him to leave Collinwood and the village."

"Would he listen to me? He claims he wants to rid

Collinwood of the evil that has come upon it."

Letty nodded with distaste. "I know he loves the estate. He's even attached to this run-down old house. But he must be persuaded to do what is best for him."

Glancing around the filthy, neglected room, Maggie responded, "I don't see how he can be satisfied here with the house so deteriorated and untidy."

"We manage."

She gave Letty a penetrating glance. "Has Barnabas ever been here before?"

The girl frowned. "Why do you ask?"

"Asa Collins' sister claims that he has. She told me to ask him about it."

Letty's face showed no expression. "Then that is what you'd better do."

"But you do know."

"I have nothing to offer on the subject. I'm sorry to have brought you out in the rain. I think I've said all I have to say."

"You're telling me to go."

Letty gave a bitter look around her. "Do you find it so inviting that you are reluctant to leave?"

"No."

"Then go. And when you talk with Barnabas again try and reason with him. And above all warn him to avoid further meetings with that girl."

"I'll do what I can," she promised. "Often when he comes to the house there is scant opportunity for us to talk."

Letty escorted her to the hall.

"I wish he wouldn't go to the main house," she said. "They all hate him."

"Is it because they fear he knows their guilty secrets?"

"More than likely." She opened the oaken door. It was still raining heavily. "Have you gotten your memory back?"

"No," Maggie said with a frown. "Sometimes I wonder if the accident ever happened. If they are not all making it up to cover the truth."

"What truth?"

"I don't know that either," she said, staring out at the rain. "But there are times when I have the weird feeling of having lived here before at a different time. Of having met Barnabas before and in a different fashion. It's like a blurred dream I can't forget."

"Remember what I said," Letty told her. "You'd be better off away from here. Barnabas as well."

"I'll remember."

She left the old house and Letty closed the stout oaken

door almost at once, not waiting to watch her on her way. Why did Letty seem so upset? What did she know that Maggie didn't? But if Letty had fears for Barnabas they were likely well founded. Without a question the little maid was being used as another pawn in the desperate game Giles and Valeria were playing.

The walk back found her in a mood of growing depression, convinced that affairs were soon likely to take a turn for the worse in the grim mansion overlooking the ocean.

At least there was no line of patients waiting to see Giles today. This was one of the most horrifying aspects of the whole dark problem at Collinwood. She didn't want to leave until a stop had been put to the mad young doctor's cruel exploitation of the consumption victims. And she was sure Barnabas felt exactly the same way.

The rain slackened as she neared the massive black hulk of the main house, but the view of the ocean was still obscured by heavy clouds. For a moment she remained on the front steps, then opened the door and went inside.

While she was still shaking the rain from her cloak, Asa Collins came up the corridor from the direction of his study and paused to glare at her.

"You must be mad to be wandering outside on a day like this," he said.

She managed a wan smile. "I have always found pleasure in the rain."

His eyes burned from under shaggy grey brows. "How well did you know my late daughter-in-law?" he demanded with a surprising abruptness.

Maggie faltered. "To be truthful I can't picture her at all. She belonged to the world of before my accident."

"That fall from Raven has served you well, hasn't it?" he suggested with some sarcasm.

She gazed at him in surprise. "I don't understand."

"I think you do," he said sternly. "For instance, it saves you offering an opinion of Olive's character—an opinion you might find it awkward to express now that she's dead."

"It is my misfortune I have lost all memory," she protested.

The old man continued to eye her coldly. "My sister Polly does not think so. It seems to her that you are deliberately pretending this loss of memory for your own purposes."

"She's wrong."

"I doubt it," the old man said sourly. "Others may think of her as doddering and senile, but I have always been impressed by her shrewdness."

"Whose shrewdness?" It was Dr. Giles Collins, his son, who

genially put this question to the old man, having suddenly made an appearance in the doorway of the living room.

Asa Collins glared at him. "It is nothing that concerns you." He wheeled around and clumped up the stairs.

Giles watched him go with a sardonic smile on his pale, sensitive face. When his father had disappeared he came across to Maggie. "My father is not in one of his best moods. We had a rather bad quarrel before you arrived."

"I'm sorry," she said, embarrassed by the revelation.

Giles shrugged. "It doesn't matter. He and I see things differently. He is still insisting I give up my clinic patients and I have refused."

"Perhaps he is right."

The young doctor stared at her in surprise. "I didn't fancy you'd take his side. I thought you were interested in humanitarian work."

"Aren't you mostly experimenting?"

"Experiments produce cures and perhaps other beneficial discoveries along the way," Giles said smoothly. "Nothing shall hinder my work in the field."

"But you've had few cures. Shouldn't you postpone your testing until you've done more work on your vaccine?"

The mad gleam showed in his eyes again. "You sound like a doubter?"

"I don't mean to. I'm thinking of the merits of caution."

"And I've been thinking of something else." He smiled. His strangely elated mood worried her. Then he added to her fears by clasping her arm in iron fingers and propelling her toward the corridor leading to the rear of the house and the door to the cellar steps and his laboratory. She tried to draw away, saying, "I'd planned to go directly to my room."

"I want you to come down to the laboratory for just a few minutes."

She had an impulse to scream, but that would have caused a ridiculous situation if his intentions were those of a harmless crank. Yet was he all that harmless? Now they were at the door to the steps and he forced her down them with him. This time he didn't even bother to pick up a candle. In his haste he plunged her into the frightening darkness.

"Please, I'm not in the mood for this," she begged.

"I need your advice badly," he insisted. "And I won't keep you long."

She barely listened to him, so great was her distress. She'd had no idea of finding herself in such a predicament. Yet this was only one of die many hazards of remaining at Collinwood. The cellar seemed damper than on her previous visit down there and she almost tripped as he guided her across to the laboratory door.

All her memories of the shadowed, littered room with its ugly operating table and pungent unpleasant odors came back with a rush as he opened the door to it. The room was dimly lighted by a single lamp on the top of a sideboard and as her eyes moved to the drapes concealing the dark anteroom she was haunted by the vision of the phantom in pink standing behind them.

Giles Collins eyed her with satisfaction as he shut the door after them and only then released his viselike hold on her arm. "Forgive my impulsiveness," he apologized. "But what I have to say is so important I couldn't chance your refusing to visit this place again."

"Please hurry with whatever it is you have to tell me," she said.

He indicated a plain chair. "Sit for a moment." He moved across the shadowed room to his desk and began rummaging in a drawer.

She sat down hesitantly, deciding it might be best to humor him. But she hoped that he wouldn't keep her there long. She wondered if she could find her way back to the stairs through the dark cellar without his help or if a scream from her could be heard above. She doubted it.

Now Giles was coming back to her, a slim dark velvet case in his hand. He stood before her with a slight smile and said, "Your accident caused a change in my plans. I had intended to speak to you about our future just when you took that bad fall. So I have postponed asking you to be my wife. Now I think it is time."

Maggie, stunned, rose to her feet. "No. It's not anything I want to discuss now."

He looked slightly disappointed. "I'm sorry," he said. "Then at least let me give you these as a present. They belonged to Olive." And he opened the velvet box to reveal a long strand of glowing pink pearls.

She stared at them in disbelief. Surely, these were the same pearls Aunt Polly had said he gave to his late wife when he had been busy persuading her to help him in his experiment—the experiment that had turned the lovely Olive into a frightening hag and brought on her death.

Shaking her head, she said in a small voice, "No. I couldn't accept any such gift."

"But I insist," Giles Collins said, taking them from the case and preparing to drape them around her neck. "Let them be a secret token of our close friendship and the promise of more happiness for us in the future."

"They're much too valuable," she protested. "And nothing is settled between us. Let us wait until later."

His mad blue eyes were fixed on her with an intentness that was frightening. "Valeria claims you have fallen in love with my cousin Barnabas and are no longer interested in me. Is that true?"

"You know I have been unwell since my accident," she protested. "I haven't had time to think of such things."

He eyed her slyly. "You haven't made any direct denial. But then I can understand your feelings. Barnabas can be charming, even though there is another dark side to him."

"I don't want to discuss it."

"I have to warn you again Barnabas and those two females in the old house are in league with the Devil. My father intends to make them leave Collinwood within a few days. He has no stomach for the things going on there."

"Barnabas has always been a gentleman to me."

Giles nodded. "You will find out what I'm saying is true. The stories about his being a vampire are founded on something more solid than imagination."

"Valeria is wrong if she claims there is a romance between Barnabas and me," she said to get him off the subject.

This seemed to please him. "That is good news. I felt you were level-headed enough not to be deceived by him. And now, if you will not accept the pearls, at least let me see them on you. Wear them for just a moment or two." She hesitated, then deciding that it might get him off the subject of Barnabas, she said, "Very well."

Giles draped the pearls around her neck and then stood back to admire them. "They were designed for a true beauty like you. One day you must consent to wear them as your own."

"They are very lovely," she acknowledged, touching her fingers to them.

"Keep them on as we talk," Giles Collins begged her. "I have a proposal to make. One that might be of great benefit to you."

"Yes?" she said in a puzzled tone.

He was rubbing his hands together in nervous agitation as he studied her with those too-bright eyes. "If you are unwilling to accept the pearls as my bride-to-be, there is a possibility you could assist me in another way and earn them for yourself."

"I don't want them!"

He raised a placating hand. "At least hear me out. As you know, I have dedicated my life to my work in this room. And I believe I am close to success with my vaccine."

"I'm glad," she said quietly.

"The purpose of the vaccine is to purify the blood. That is why I have been testing it on those unfortunate souls whose lungs are being devoured by consumption. If I can clear up their diseased blood they should recover."

"I see," Maggie lied tensely. She couldn't imagine how all this concerned her.

His eyes narrowed. "Just now I want to do a series of carefully controlled experiments on a different sort of person, one whose body is not corrupted by disease, but pure and young. You could give me the aid I so badly need by offering yourself for doses of my vaccine."

The horror of the suggestion was overwhelming. Earn the necklace as Olive had, at the cost of her looks and her life! She reached up with frantic fingers to unlock the clasp. "Please," she begged. "Take it off!" It had come to signify captivity and terror for her.

Giles Collins listened to her pleas calmly. "Now, really," he said, "I think it suits you perfectly."

She had found the catch and opened it. Dropping the pearls in her palm, she offered them to him. "I'm sorry. I dislike pearls."

"Odd," he observed as he accepted them and placed them in the case once again. "Most women like them only second to diamonds."

"I have to go to my room now." She moved towards the door.

He followed her. "You didn't answer my question? Will you assist me in my work here?"

She daren't speak out what was in her mind. If he was as mad as she suspected, he might attack her. So she took what she hoped might be a better way. "It's an important move for me to consider. I'll need some time to think it over."

"Take some time if you like," he agreed. "But I can't delay too long."

"I realize that."

"And please don't mention this to anyone else," Giles Collins said. "It is very personal with me. I'd especially not want you to tell Barnabas."

"I understand," she said. "Will you be continuing your experiments with the consumptives in the meantime?"

He nodded. "Oh, I must go on treating them. Poor souls! They expect it."

And then he opened the door and saw her safely up the stairs. She was trembling as she stepped out into the hall, but somehow she controlled her feelings enough that he seemed not to notice. One thing was clear to her now: the role Giles Collins had planned for her when he'd had her brought to Collinwood. She was to follow in Olive's footsteps as an offering to his madness.

The rain tapered off to a drizzle towards evening. Maggie spent a good portion of the waning day in her room. It wasn't until dinner time that she joined the others downstairs. And the brooding tension which had come over the big house was clearly evident as they gathered at the long dining table in the richly paneled room.

The flickering candles in their silver holders gave a luxurious glow to the white-clothed table with its fine china. Old Asa Collins presided over the meal in his usual aloof fashion. Aunt Polly seemed in a good mood and several times actually offered Maggie a conspiratorial smile. This made her uneasy since she felt that Valeria and Giles were watching both her and the old woman closely.

As usual they gathered in the front parlor for coffee and the men had after-dinner brandy. They were only there for a short time when Barnabas Collins joined them.

Aunt Polly was the first to greet him. "What a pleasant surprise, Barnabas. Will you have a brandy or perhaps a liqueur?"

"Neither, thank you," he told her with a grave smile. "I have come by chiefly for the company after the gloomy day we've had."

Giles, who was standing with Valeria, took on a knowing look. "I should think this somber weather would please you. Anyone who can be satisfied to five in the old house must enjoy the dank and gloomy."

Barnabas gave him a disdainful glance. "I have an appreciation of the ancient," he said. "I doubt if you'd understand my feelings in this regard."

Valeria smiled mockingly. "I suppose it would be hard for us to see things through your viewpoint. It's bound to be very different."

To Maggie it seemed that beneath the casual pleasantries there was a kind of duel going on. If this was true Barnabas was holding his own in excellent fashion. Gradually he moved away from the others so that he and she had a comer of the room to themselves.

Keeping an eye on Giles and Valeria, who were standing before the blazing log fire at the end of the room, Barnabas said, "I understand you saw Letty this afternoon."

She looked up into his solemn face. "Yes, I did. She asked me to come over."

"And you told her that you had seen Mabel going out to keep a rendezvous with me?"

Maggie blushed. "I didn't think there was any harm in

telling the truth."

His deep-set eyes were fixed on hers. "Letty is worrying too much. She sees danger where it may not exist."

"She is only thinking of your welfare."

"I know that," he agreed, still taking an occasional glance at the two by the fireplace. "She's certain that Giles and Valeria are up to some fiendish business and arranging it so I'll be blamed."

"They are not above it."

He smiled faindy. "You have made some discoveries on your own?"

"I'd like to leave here as soon as I can manage it," she said. "I'm afraid. I don't know what's going on but I'm sure Letty is right. It's something horrible."

"I'd prefer it if you wouldn't mention Mabel's name again to anyone. Not even to Letty. The girl has been of great help to me and she could suffer for her friendliness."

"Very well," she agreed. "But listen. When I came back from the old house this afternoon Giles insisted I go down to his laboratory with him. And while I was there he tried to talk me into helping him with his experiment."

For the first time since his arrival Barnabas seemed concerned. "You mustn't have anything to do with that vaccine business. You know what happened to Olive."

"Too well," she said gravely. "He was so fanatical about it he scared me. I handled the situation as best I could by telling him I'd think it over."

"He'll continue to bother you."

"I realize that," she said. "Luckily I always have the excuse that I'm still unwell after my accident."

Barnabas was studying her thoughtfully. "How much do you remember now?"

"Not any more than I did in the beginning," she said. "I still feel differently about you than any of the others. It seems that I know you better. And it's somehow part of what went on before I came out of my coma following the accident. That doesn't make sense, does it?"

"I wouldn't worry about it," was his reply. "I think I'd better leave now. I have things to look into and I don't want them to get the idea we're too friendly."

"Whatever you like," she sighed. "The other evening you suggested I stay on here so that an end could be put to the dreadful hoax of the clinic. Do you still feel the same way? That my remaining here can help stifle the evil at Collinwood?"

"I hope so," he said sincerely. "It is still early for me to be certain. If you'll be patient for a few more days we should see the pattern unfold."

"Letty thinks you are wrong, that we should both go away from Collinsport."

"Letty does not have the same interest in the place that I have," he said quietly. "It is her first visit here."

Maggie raised her eyebrows. "That brings up a question I've wanted to ask you. Have you been here before?"

"We can talk about that later," he said. "I must go." And he went across to where Asa Collins and Aunt Polly were seated and said goodnight to them in his courtly fashion. Then he nodded to the other two who were still talking quietly by the fireplace.

Maggie joined Barnabas as he started out. Her admiration for the tall, handsome Britisher was as strong as ever. His broad shoulders carried his caped coat with distinction and he swung his black cane with its silver wolf's head in the manner of a born gentleman. His serious, sallow face still struck her as aristocratic.

As they neared the door leading to the hallway they passed a huge mirror with an ornate gold frame. She glanced into it and caught her breath. For while the mirror clearly showed her reflection the man at her side did not appear in it at all. Barnabas was a vampire!

CHAPTER 9

Barnabas must have noticed her shock, for he looked at her with a questioning glance. "Is something wrong?" They had emerged into the shadows of the entrance hallway. She was still feeling the impact of her eerie experience; it took her a moment or two to begin to rationalize it. With the first fright over now she began to see that it had probably only been a trick of vision.

The chances were that it was the angle at which she'd looked into the mirror that had produced the odd illusion. This handsome man at her side couldn't be one of those who rose from their coffins in the night to slake their thirst for human blood!

"What is wrong?" Barnabas repeated his question with more concern.

She managed to dismiss the sudden mood of fear and depression that had temporarily engulfed her. With a small tragic smile, she said, "It's nerves, mostly. I suppose this miserable day has left me in a bad state."

"Nothing more than that?" His deep-set eyes were fixed on her.

"Nothing more than that."

"Remember what I have told you."

"I'll try. I'm very weary of it here."

Barnabas looked sympathetic. "I can well understand that," he agreed. "It will only be a little while longer. Until then, be patient." He bent close and touched his cold lips to her forehead and offered her a parting smile.

As she waited in the open doorway, watching him stride off into the wet darkness she had a feeling that Letty's warning should not be dismissed lightly. Barnabas could be in real danger.

"He has won you over, hasn't he?" It was Giles Collins who had quietly come up behind her to make the comment.

She gave him a frightened glance over her shoulder. "I didn't realize you had come out here."

Giles' smile was unpleasant. "I'm sure of that. Otherwise you'd have spared me that touching farewell between you two."

Maggie shut the door and turned to start back to the parlor. "I don't think it's any of your business."

"Not even when I happen to care for you?"

"I thought we'd settled that."

"Nothing is settled yet," he promised her. "And I vow you'll have a change of heart when you discover the truth about Barnabas."

Silently she pressed on to the parlor where she found Valeria and Aunt Polly sitting on the divan together and old Asa Collins standing gloomily not far from the doorway, his eyes fixed on one of the many portraits decorating the elegant, big room. She went over to stand beside him and saw that the portrait hung there was of Barnabas. It gave her a start.

She said, "I had no idea you had a painting of Barnabas."

Asa Collins gave her a condescending glance. "It's a portrait of Barnabas Collins, well enough. But not a portrait of the man who left here."

"It looks exactly like him," she said in surprise.

"I was just thinking the same thing," old Asa Collins admitted. "But this portrait was done years ago. It's a study of the first Barnabas Collins and dates back to the late eighteenth century."

Maggie gave her attention to the painting again. "Then he is the one who left Collinwood to live in England."

"Yes," Asa Collins said. "And if all the accounts are true he left here under a cloud. A bad penny like this fellow who has come back here to visit."

She attempted no direct argument. Instead, she said, "I think the portrait shows a strong face."

"He was mixed up with some evil doings," Asa Collins told her. "And I have decided his portrait shall hang in this room no more. I'm having it taken down and stored away in the attic."

"But it's a fine painting," she protested. "The room is richer because of it."

"And I'm vexed every time it catches my eye," Asa Collins grumbled. "Indeed, the only thing my son and I can agree upon is our mutual dislike for the present Barnabas." With this he marched off huffily.

Maggie remained in the parlor only a few minutes longer before returning upstairs to her own room. As usual, the rain had ended in a heavy mist. She could barely see the tall trees at the edge of the grounds from her window. Wearily she prepared for bed, thinking how things had changed for her in the grim mansion.

In the beginning she had accepted them all at face value. Aunt Polly had seemed a somewhat sour, stout old woman with only a minor interest in what was going on. Pale, blond Dr. Giles Collins had been the epitome of the grieving widower and kindly doctor, whose career, interrupted by the tragic demise of his lovely young wife, had turned to ministering to the needs of the afflicted in a free clinic. Valeria, dark and lovely, had perfectly fitted the role of adoring sister-in-law and good friend, anxious to help Giles regain an interest in living. And old Asa Collins had appeared the dour patriarch of the house with little tolerance or sympathy.

Now that the masks had been ripped away from the principal characters in this weird drama, it was Asa Collins who came off best. At least the old man was honest in his beliefs and didn't try to win sympathy by pretending to be a different sort of person. And Aunt Polly had at times shown herself to be shrewd and sympathetic. But Giles Collins had gradually revealed himself to be sly and bitter, and his vaunted interest in caring for consumptives was nothing more than a cover for some kind of weird experiment. He was obsessed to the point of madness with this dark venture in his laboratory.

Valeria no longer held Maggie's trust. Despite the girl's lovely face and friendly manner, she suspected that Valeria could be behind most of the evil schemes being concocted under the roof of the old mansion.

And what of the dead Olive, Valeria's equally beautiful sister, whose death was so ghastly that her husband had bricked up the entrance to her room as a way to seal off the tragic memories? Asa Collins had suggested she had been less than perfect. Aunt Polly had revealed that there had been frequent quarrels between Olive and Giles, and that Giles had bribed his wife to subject herself to his weird experiments with the same pearls he'd only that afternoon offered her for the same purpose. Maggie found he was repeating himself in a frightening way.

Aunt Polly contended they had brought Maggie to the old house by the sea for a purpose, that Giles and Valeria had some horrible game to play out in which she'd have a role. But what was it?

With this disquieting question, she put out the lamp and went to bed. Exhausted, she fell asleep almost immediately—and wakened later with the same abruptness. Staring into the darkness, she at once saw the reason for her waking. The terrifying phantom in pink was slowly approaching her bedside.

The sheer hatred showing on the withered, haglike face of the apparition froze Maggie's scream in her throat. She shrank back against the pillows as the figure of terror advanced, its bony hands outstretched and menacing. She was smothered by the odor of death and decay. The skeleton fingers found her throat; their pressure increased relentlessly. There was no longer any hope of her enlisting aid. She now fought to free herself from the murderous hands and remain conscious. It was a losing battle.

When she opened her eyes the same withered face was staring down at her. At her look of terror, the hag gestured for her to remain silent. She did, gazing up at the face of the wrinkled, toothless crone and trying to place it. Something was . . . different.

Then she remembered. It was Mrs. Judd, Barnabas' housekeeper. The old woman had her usual shawl over her head and she carried a stubby, dripping candle whose wavering flame highlighted her witch-like countenance.

The old woman croaked, "I was afraid you might be dead, dearie."

Maggie raised herself on an elbow warily. Had it been Mrs. Judd who'd attacked her? The face of the old woman was remarkably similar to that of the phantom.

Her throat ached as she asked, "How long have you been in this room?"

"I just came," the old woman said. "I found the door ajar and I wanted to see if you knew anything about Barnabas."

Maggie, still suspicious, lifted a hand to her burning throat. "Why should I know anything about him?"

"Miss Letty said he planned to come here and see you tonight."

"He was here ages ago."

"Did he not tell you where he was going?" The eyes buried in the wrinkled face were appraising her.

Maggie shook her head. "No," she said, close to anger. "Just before you came in I saw a ghost—a ghost resembling you, and it choked me into unconsciousness."

The hag's face was unrevealing in the candlelight. "I know nothing about it."

She frowned. "But you must! You should have seen her! She was all in pink!"

"I didn't see anything but the door ajar," the old woman maintained. "And I must be getting back to Miss Letty."

"How did you get in the house?"

Mrs. Judd grinned slyly. "I have ways." She turned and hurried out of the room, shutting the door after her.

Left in darkness again Maggie was seized by terror. She frantically fumbled for a match and touched it to the lamp's wick. She relaxed a very little with the lamplight to bolster her assurance. But she doubted that she would sleep again for the balance of the night.

The unexpected arrival of Mrs. Judd must have saved her life by putting the phantom to rout. Unless, of course, Mrs. Judd was the phantom. It would take her only seconds to slip off the robe of pink and appear as herself. It was a possibility not to be dismissed without more thought.

But why should the witch-like housekeeper attack her? There was no reasonable explanation.

She lay back on the pillow and gazed up at the protecting canopy with worried eyes. Why had Letty sent the old woman to question her about Barnabas at this time of night? There had to be some urgent reason. And again she experienced the depression and fears she'd known earlier in the evening.

Morning came at last and it was gray and foggy. From the distant town came the monotonous warning of the Collinsport foghorn. Maggie got up early, still tormented by the savage attack made on her during the night. She knew it would be useless to complain about it to any of the others in the house; they would only put it down to her vivid imagination.

Yet the faint red marks on her throat proved that more than lively imaginings were involved. She studied them in the dresser mirror with some concern. She meant to tell Barnabas about her frightening experience and seek his advice. Which brought to mind Mrs. Judd's visit and the question of where Barnabas had gone last night.

By the time she was dressed a maid appeared with her breakfast. She asked, "Where is Mabel?"

The girl gave her an uneasy glance. "I'm filling in for her this morning."

"Oh?" Maggie lifted her eyebrows. "Is she ill?"

"I don't know, miss." The maid hurried out.

Maggie sat down to her breakfast mystified by the girl's attitude. But she dismissed it as the behavior of a shy village girl. They were often reluctant to engage in small talk with strangers.

After she finished eating, she started downstairs to see if she could find Aunt Polly in the rear parlor. The old woman often spent her mornings there. But when she reached the bottom of the stairs she found Asa Collins and Constable Withers in serious discussion.

The two men abruptly halted their conversation when they saw her and exchanged a troubled glance that warned her something more than the ordinary had gone wrong.

Asa Collins came forward to greet her. The old man was

scowling. "I'm glad you came down, Miss Evans," he said. "I was at the point of calling you."

"Indeed?"

Asa turned partly to the constable and said, "Constable Withers made an alarming discovery this morning. He found the dead body of the girl, Mabel, in a ditch at the junction of the Collinwood road with the main highway."

"Mabel!" she gasped, a hand rising to her throat.

Withers nodded gravely. "Sorry to break the news to you this way, miss. But we've had to tell all the household, since it's possible one or another of you may be able to help us."

Asa Collins was regarding her in his sternest fashion. "The girl was your maid," he said. "You must have had some conversations with her."

"No," she said. "Actually we talked very little."

"I find that hard to believe," the old man said. "Did she tell you she was a friend of Barnabas Collins?"

"His name was never mentioned between us."

"But you must have known that she often went out at night to meet him," Asa Collins insisted.

This was another matter. "She could have. I wouldn't be sure of that."

"Other girls in service here have told us this was true," Constable Withers said. "And the condition of her body when we found it has made us suspicious of this man from England."

Maggie clung to the post at the foot of the stairs, wondering if she was going to faint.

Asa Collins said, "To put it bluntly, Miss Evans, the girl's body had been drained of blood."

Withers nodded forlornly. "I have never encountered a case like it before."

Asa gave him a disgusted glance. "You have never had to deal with a vampire before. And I'm convinced that is what my cousin from England happens to be."

Maggie had to speak up for him. "You're not being fair, Mr. Collins. I'm sure Barnabas had nothing to do with it."

He turned on her. "How can you be sure?" he snapped.

She gestured futilely. "I know Barnabas well enough to be certain he's not a murderer."

"Rather unconvincing evidence," the old man said with disgust. "You'll have to come up with something better than that to cause us to change our minds."

Constable Withers stepped forward and looked at her with suspicion. "It would be best to help us if you can, miss."

"There's nothing I can offer except my good opinion of

Barnabas."

The constable tugged at a side-whisker. "Well, now, miss, since you and the gentleman are such good friends he must have told you a lot about himself."

"Not really."

"Did he ever give you any reason to suspect he wasn't a normal man?"

The memory of the mirror without the reflection of Barnabas where it should have been came back to haunt her. But she reminded herself that she'd already found a solution for that vexing discovery. She'd looked into the mirror from an odd angle. "I have always been much impressed by him as a fine, English gentleman."

Asa Collins eyed her coldly. "What about his holing himself up in that old house with those two females? And his showing himself only after dusk? Don't you consider that an odd way to behave?"

"He has good reasons for both those tilings," she reminded Asa Collins.

"Trumped-up reasons," the old man snorted. "It is a known fact that vampires rest in their coffins in the daylight hours and in the darkness stalk the living for blood. I say that Mabel fell victim to such a monster in the person of Barnabas."

Maggie tried to maintain a calm front. "Why don't you question him?"

Constable Withers looked unhappy. "We've tried, but they— Letty and the old woman—refuse to let us speak to him until later in the day."

"You should have forced your way in," Asa Collins told the man. "It is my property and you have my permission."

"Yet your cousin is the tenant," Constable Withers said. "And I dislike resorting to violence if I can avoid it."

"Are you willing to wait for more girls to be found murdered and bloodless before you act?"

"No, sir. I shall see him within the next few hours." And to her he added, "There is nothing more you can tell us, miss?"

"I'm afraid I'm unable to help in any way."

"I see," the constable said. "Well, that will be all for now, miss. But if you think of anything you may have missed, don't hesitate to get in touch with me."

"I won't," she promised ambiguously.

She tried to slip away, but Asa stopped her. "I warn you that until this matter is cleared up I shall continue to believe Barnabas guilty. And if the law allows him to remain at large I shall forbid him entrance to Collinwood."

"I hope you are not making a hasty decision," she commented quietly and withdrew.

But her calm words did not represent the entire state of her heart or mind. She was in a kind of panic for the handsome man she'd come to be so fond of. The dark rumors of witchcraft in the old house, along with the hint that he was a vampire, would all work against him now.

She doubted that the constable would reach him before dusk. Barnabas would maintain his usual pattern and not show himself until then, and the two women say nothing. But eventually Barnabas would have to account for his movements last night. Would he be able to do it satisfactorily? That was why Mrs. Judd had made the weird midnight call on her. Letty had known something dreadful had happened.

The brutal fact was that Mabel was dead, murdered in a peculiarly atrocious fashion. Why would anyone have wanted to drain the body of all its blood, unless the murderer was a vampire? It was a frightening thought.

For once she was grateful for the shadows of the hallway on this gray day. The near-darkness gave her a feeling of privacy as she attempted to grapple with her inner turmoil. And by the time she reached the rear parlor the worst of her panic had left her. She was almost grateful to see Aunt Polly placidly seated and busy with her knitting needles.

The old woman paused to greet her. "Have you heard about Mabel?"

"Yes," she said in a low voice, taking a chair almost directly across from the stout woman.

Aunt Polly leaned forward. "I wasn't surprised."

"You weren't?"

"No," the old woman said with satisfaction. "I've felt something dreadful like this was going to happen for a long while." She sighed. "Still, I do think it a pity it had to be Mabel."

Maggie frowned with disbelief. "How could you possibly predict the murder?"

"Because of the curse." The eyes in the brown, wrinkled face were bright.

"What curse?"

"The Norris curse," the old woman exclaimed with a note of triumph.

"You mentioned that once before, but I didn't understand—and I still don't. What are you talking about?" Maybe Giles and Valeria were right; the old woman was insane. What possible connection could there be between the murder of the pretty maid and a curse on the family of Valeria Norris?

Aunt Polly was looking immensely pleased with herself. "You're afraid for Barnabas, aren't you?"

"I suppose I am," she admitted frankly. "Your brother is making wild accusations against him."

Aunt Polly nodded. "I know. Asa is a bad one when he gets an idea in his head. And he's never liked Barnabas. So he won't admit that the curse is shadowing Collinwood."

"What curse are you talking about? And how does it bear on Barnabas? What kind of curse?"

"It has a bearing on us all," the old woman said, returning to her knitting. "You'll find out about it soon enough."

"If you know anything that will help solve the crime, you should speak up."

Aunt Polly didn't lift her head from her knitting. "There will be more murders. Count on it. And you'd do better to worry about your own safety than fret for Barnabas. He'll take care of himself."

"You sound so sure."

"My left eye has been watering," the old woman murmured. "It is a sure sign of misfortune. And they ask for evil here by sweeping the floors at night. Such sweeping disturbs the spirits of the dead."

Maggie rose in disgust. "Whatever makes you believe in such things?"

Aunt Polly paused with her knitting needles again to give her a wise look. "You believe in the phantom in pink."

It was an unexpected and meaningless reply, as far as she was concerned. She said, "I'd hoped you might be able to help me. But it seems I was wrong." And she left Aunt Polly alone to continue her knitting.

As Maggie hurried out into the hallway she almost bumped into Valeria, who halted and said, "Isn't it awful about Mabel?"

"Yes."

"The whole place is in a turmoil," Valeria continued. "Constable Withers and his men are questioning everyone. Did he talk with you?"

"A little while ago."

"I had to answer his questions as well," Valeria sighed.

"And now he is down in the laboratory bothering Giles. And Giles feels badly enough about this as it is. He's going to cancel his clinic today because of what has happened."

"I can understand his feelings."

"Is Aunt Polly in there?" Valeria asked, indicating the rear parlor with a nod.

"Yes," Maggie said. "She seems to be very confused."

"The news of the murder bothered her that way," Valeria said. "She hasn't been well lately. Asa is worried about her."

"He would be," she said politely, anxious to be on her way.

But Valeria appeared in no hurry to allow her to go. She said, "You know who is the chief suspect in the crime?"

"I haven't any idea," Maggie said stoutly, knowing Valeria was bound to mention Barnabas.

And she did. "Barnabas, of course! Didn't the constable tell you?"

"I think his name was mentioned."

"They have a fairly strong case against him," Valeria went on. "One of the other maids who was a close friend of Mabel's claims that Mabel went out regularly at night to meet Barnabas."

"Sometimes girls are apt to exaggerate at times like this."

"And that isn't all," Valeria said, ignoring her comment. "This girl claims that always when Mabel returned to her room she appeared dazed and weak. And there was a strange red mark on her throat that often took hours to vanish completely."

Maggie held her breath. She mustn't show any sign of lack of faith in Barnabas. "So?" Her voice was thin.

"There's only one explanation," Valeria said with assurance. "It was the mark of a vampire. So Barnabas must truly be one. And in the end he became so greedy for her blood that he drained every ounce of it from her poor body."

Determined to conceal her alarm, Maggie said, "I know nothing of such things."

"Consider yourself lucky. And count on it that you will learn more before this is over."

"Couldn't the murderer have been a stranger? Someone passing through the village?"

"Giles doesn't think so and neither do I," Valeria said. "But then, knowing how you feel about Barnabas, I can't expect you to face up to this in a sensible fashion."

She felt her cheeks burn. "I think we will all be more rational in our theories when the first shock of this wears away." And she turned and left the dark girl standing there.

Continuing on to the front hallway, she debated what she would do. One thing was clear. She should see Letty and talk with her, regardless of what the others thought or felt. At this time she could do no less than declare herself for Barnabas and the two females of his household.

After going upstairs briefly for her cloak, she made her way along the path leading to the old house. It was still wet and the grass was high in places so she had to pick her steps. She'd seen the constable's carriage waiting in front of the house and knew he must still be down in the laboratory with Giles. She wondered what the constable thought of the young doctor. Probably considered him a benefactor to the poor and ill, since he wouldn't guess the truth of what was going on there. Nor would he be apt to believe her if she told him.

Arriving at the old house, she at once went up the front steps and knocked on the ancient oak door. As she stood waiting she was sure she heard a sound from a nearby window, and she sensed unseen eyes studying her from behind the shutters. Finally the door was opened partway on a chain and Mrs. Judd peered out at her.

"It will do you no good to ask to see Mr. Barnabas," Mrs. Judd said adamantly. "He isn't here."

"I want to speak to Letty for just a moment."

"She's poorly. You'd best go back to Collinwood and stay there."

"No," Maggie said sharply. "Please tell her I'm here. I know she'll see me."

Mrs. Judd scowled. "I'll tell her, but it won't make any difference." And she shut the door again.

Maggie stood there feeling unsure of herself or what she'd say to the girl when she saw her. The fog was almost as wet as rain. She pulled the cloak tightly around her and stared back in the direction of Collinwood. At least no one had followed her.

There were footsteps approaching on the other side of the door and then the door opened and Letty was standing there. Her attractive face was pale and lined with worry. She said, "I guessed you'd come."

"I want to help Barnabas any way I can."

Letty eyed her worriedly. "Yes," she said, "I believe you do."

"That is why I came here. To ask your advice."

"Come inside a moment." Letty unhooked the chain so she could enter the damp, shadowed hall, then put the chain back on its hook. "I'm careful to use this today in case they might decide to force their way in."

Maggie searched the other girl's face. "It wouldn't do them any good, would it? Mrs. Judd said Barnabas isn't here."

"He's not far away," Letty assured her. "The idea of those people saying he murdered Mabel. He was very fond of the girl. He wouldn't dream of ever harming her."

"I believe that," she said unhappily, "but not another person at Collinwood appears to. And I assume that will go for the village as well."

The darkness of the hallway made it hard for her to read Letty's face, but she could tell the blonde was upset by the tone in which she spoke. She said, "I had a long talk with Barnabas late last night. After Mrs. Judd went to ask you about him. He came back less than an hour later. And he told me he left Mabel early in the evening."

"Has he any way of proving it?"

"I think so," Letty said. "He took her to the Blue Whale, the tavern near the docks. The crew of a Norwegian ship was there. A tall sailor among them named Olaf spoke English very well. Mabel liked him and Barnabas left her with him. Whatever happened to her took place after that."

Maggie felt a thrill of hope. "Then if we find the Norwegian we can prove Barnabas is innocent."

"We might be able to," Letty agreed. "But I can't leave here. And even if I did risk going into the village and leaving the house in Grandmother's care, there's no promise that I'd find that Olaf. The ship may have sailed with him on it."

"Surely we'll be luckier than that," Maggie said. "Let me go. I can get a carriage at the house."

"Do you think they'd allow you to go into Collinsport? Especially if they know why you're going."

"I won't tell them."

"Do you really think you can manage it?"

"I will."

"Good girl," the blonde said. "The bartender knows Barnabas well. Talk to him and he may be able to locate that Olaf."

"I'll go at once." She left Letty and hurried back along the path to Collinwood. She'd decided to go straight to the stables and ask for a small carriage to drive herself into the village.

She was close to the grim old mansion with its tall chimneys when she saw a gaunt, poorly-dressed woman coming running to meet her. As the woman came near her, Maggie saw that she had the emaciated features and high color spots on the cheeks so common among Giles' patients. The woman was undoubtedly one of those attending his clinic.

"Please help me, miss! You must help me!" the woman gasped.

Maggie stared at her sympathetically. "I'm sorry, Dr. Collins is not having a clinic today. You may have heard. One of our maids was murdered last night. We're all very upset."

"I know about that," the woman said hysterically. "The woman at the door said there was no clinic and the doctor wouldn't be able to see me. But I have to see him. Something terrible has happened."

She saw the horror written on the woman's thin face. "What is your trouble?" she asked gently.

The gaunt woman was clutching at her arm now. "It's my baby! My little seven-year-old girl! She has this cursed plague like the rest of us." The woman paused to cough rackingly. "The doctor has been giving her his medicine. And early this morning some awful spell took hold of her. She's withering and aging each hour. It's as though she is becoming an old woman. I've heard whispers of it happening to others but I didn't believe it. And now it's my little girl. And if he doesn't do something she'll die before the day is out like the rest of them. Please, miss! Talk to him for me!"

Maggie felt ill. Had Giles hit on some means of artificially aging an individual overnight? And was he perfecting it with tests on these unfortunate souls?

In a tight tone, she said, "I don't understand what the trouble is. But I will try to get Dr. Collins to see you."

The woman clasped Maggie's hand. "Heaven bless you!" she exclaimed. "It's my darling's life is at stake. I couldn't believe it when they shut the door in my face."

"As I said, everyone is very upset," Maggie told her. "Now please come along with me."

The woman hurried along at her side, breaking into a heart-rending cough every so often. The exertion and emotional drain were obviously costing the distraught mother heavily. At last they came to the side door leading to the cellar. Maggie went down the several steps and pounded on the door with its small glass pane. She had to knock with force several times before Giles' pale, sensitive face showed in the tiny window. He wore a scowl until he saw it was her and then his expression changed to one of surprise.

Opening the door at once, he asked, "What is wrong? What are you doing here?" On seeing the gaunt woman behind her, his expression changed to one of wariness.

Maggie glanced around. "This woman's child is very ill. She thinks it could be a reaction to some sort of medicine you've given her. It's urgent. So I told her I'd try and get you to see her."

"Please, doctor!" The woman pushed forward.

Giles looked trapped and uneasy. "Very well," he said. "I'll fix you up something to give the little girl. Come into my office for a moment."

Maggie gave him an approving look.

"Thank you." Giles said, "I want to see you. Wait a minute."

"I'll be back shortly," she promised. And without giving him a chance to reply she hurried back up the steps and headed around the comer of the mansion to the stables.

The elderly groom knew her, but he still rubbed his chin uneasily at her for a horse and carriage to drive to the village. She said, "I'll only be gone a short while."

"That's not it, miss," the groom explained. "It's just that I don't know whether Mr. Asa would approve of it or not."

"It's all right," Maggie said, drawing on her imagination. "He told me I could ask you for a carriage whenever I liked. He doesn't want me to ride in the saddle again because of my accident."

This seemed to convince the old man. He looked brighter. "The master is right in that. Raven is a fair devil when he wants to be. I don't reckon you'll be picking him for the carriage?"

"No. Something a good deal less spirited."

"Aye. I have just the one. A brown mare as gentle as a kitten."

Maggie drew a deep sigh of relief. She had been in luck thus far; surely her luck would hold the rest of the way. Asa Collins had left late for his office in the village and wouldn't be back until evening. Giles was occupied with the mother of the stricken child—though that mightn't be for long. And she could only pray that Valeria wouldn't look out the window and see her at the stables.

Within ten minutes she was seated in the carriage and flicking the reins for the docile brown mare to take her into the village. The carriage jogged over the rough road and soon she turned a bend and the towering structure of Collinwood was out of sight. Maggie felt a little easier and began to make her plans for this venture into the town.

First, she would go to the Blue Whale. If she was lucky, the bartender would be able to tell her where to find the Norwegian.

As the carriage wheels creaked over the wet surface of the road and she strained her eyes to peer through the fog, she began to worry about Giles. She doubted very much if he had an antidote for the condition he'd induced with his vaccine. And she felt a surging pity for the poor mother. Surely there must be another doctor in Collinsport. She would ask at the Blue Whale. And if there should be one, she'd try to call on him briefly as well.

Within twenty minutes she came to the outskirts of the fishing village. The main street was on a hill and ran straight down to the docks. The Blue Whale tavern was located midway down the street and on the left side.

Maggie grasped her skirt so that she might make the long step down from the carriage with safety. Then she tied the reins to keep the mare from bolting off in her absence and went into the Blue Whale. The tavern was empty on this foggy morning and only the proprietor himself, a pleasant gray-haired man, lounged behind the bar in his shirtsleeves.

He heard her story out with polite interest. "Aye, that is right. Barnabas did bring the girl here. But later she began to joke with the Norwegian and give all her attention to him. Poor Mabel was always a bit of a flirt. So Barnabas, being a true gent, paid his bill and left."

"So the girl was here with this Olaf?"

"For a good hour and a half they were together. It wasn't a busy night, so I had time to notice and say a word to them every little while. Then she seemed to change her mind about liking Olaf. I saw her going over to sit with a couple of the local lads. The next thing I knew she had gone, either with one of the boys from around here or on her own. Olaf was upset when he found she'd left without him even saying goodbye."

"Is the Norwegian's ship still here?"

"Sorry, miss. They sailed this morning. That's why Olaf was feeling so bad."

Maggie sighed dejectedly. "That news makes me feel bad as

well. I wanted him as a witness for Barnabas."

The bartender looked astounded. "They trying to blame Barnabas Collins for Mabel's murder?"

Her eyes met his. "Of course. Didn't you expect it? You must have heard some of the wicked rumors they've been spreading about him."

"I know," the big man agreed angrily. "And it isn't right. Barnabas is a fine man. They don't like him here because he has manners and dignity."

She reconsidered. "Perhaps we'll be all right even without Olaf, providing you are willing to go to Constable Withers and tell him just what you told me."

"Glad to. I would have done it before if I'd figured they were going to try and blame Barnabas Collins. I'll sure give the constable an earful."

"You don't know how grateful I am," she said with a warm smile.

"It's nothing. I always try to be fair."

"I'm sure you do," she said. "Now there's one more thing. Is there a doctor in the village? I mean besides Dr. Giles Collins."

He looked disgusted. "That Giles Collins isn't any real doctor. He never has done anything but run that clinic. And my guess is he's killed more than he's cured."

"I'm afraid you could be right," she said grimly.

"The doctor we rely on in the district is old Dr. West. He lives in the big white house up on the hill as you first come into town. That's where you can find him when he isn't out on call."

Again Maggie was lucky. She found the big white house on the hill without difficulty and Dr. West was in his office. He was a thin, mild-mannered man with a stoop and a white mustache. He looked grave as he heard her story.

"I've been wondering about what's been going on out there," he said, after he finished. "I'm not one to interfere. But people have come to me with strange stories. And I've been called in to attend two or three dying children who looked more like old men and women than youngsters."

Maggie stared at him worriedly. "I'm sure the change in them was caused by something more than the mere ravages of their disease."

"They all had consumption," the old doctor agreed. "And it can be pretty awful. But I do agree that the cases I saw looked more than thin and wasted from disease. They looked as if they'd died of premature old age."

"He has some kind of vaccine he's obsessed with. What it may be terrifies me."

"I don't like it myself," Dr. West admitted, "but as I say, I'm not one to go barging into another man's practice."

"Surely there's something you can do. Something is very wrong. If you could find some way to make him stop this clinic it would be a blessing."

Dr. West nodded gravely. "I feel responsibility. People around here have looked to me for medical advice for near a half-century. I guess they'd want me to speak up if I thought something was wrong."

"I'm sure of it."

"But the Collins family is a respected one. And I've wanted to give him every chance. I've been hoping his clinic would halt the spread of the consumption that has been raging through whole families in the county. I guess I was hoping for too much."

"You must go out and at least question him."

"All right, young lady, you've convinced me," Dr. West said. "I'll see him. It may not be for a day or so. But you say he's closed the clinic temporarily on account of the murder. So that gives me extra time."

She rose. "Just don't forget about it. Doctor. He's bound to start those horrible experiments again."

"I'm not likely to forget," the old man assured her as he got to his feet. "I don't want anything like that on my conscience."

She drove back to Collinwood feeling much more hopeful. When this crisis had come to an end, she would consult Dr. West again, about herself this time. She would tell him of her accident and the loss of memory and ask his advice about returning to Boston.

As the mare placidly jogged along through the fog Maggie tried to recall something of the life she had known in Boston. No, there was nothing. Except for the vague feeling she'd been at Collinwood in another time and that she'd known Barnabas then, her mind was still a blank. It was as if her life had begun after her fall from Raven's saddle.

The fog showed no sign of clearing. Often at this time of year it could remain foggy for days. As she came nearer to the estate her spirits fell. There would be questions; and, undoubtedly, annoyance at her temerity in taking this drive into town. She decided she should have some sort of explanation and it seemed her visit to the old doctor might serve.

After she'd returned the mare and carriage and went around to enter the front door she was ready for the encounter that followed. Giles was standing in the hallway with an angry expression on his sensitive face. "Where have you been?"

She replied calmly, "To the village."

"I know that," he snapped. "The groom said you asked him for transportation. I want to know where you went in the village?"

Her eyes met his. "To see Dr. West."

"Dr. West?" He looked surprised, almost frightened. "What did you go to see him for? I'm a doctor. Why didn't you come to me?"

"You have enough on your mind as it is, and I wanted another medical opinion on my accident and its effects. I was feeling very bad. That's what made me decide to make the visit."

He eyed her suspiciously. "He's an old fuddy-duddy. Completely out of touch with new advances in medicine."

She shrugged. "Perhaps so. I can only tell you his opinion was the same as your own."

Giles looked brighter. "Indeed!"

"So it seems I'll just have to wait for my stupid memory to return. He agreed it could take a long while."

Giles lost all his anger. With a smile on his pale face he came close and took her by the arms. "You don't know the agonies I suffered when I heard you'd ridden off. I was afraid you might have made the error of leaving for good."

"I wouldn't do that without telling you," she said, watching those over-bright eyes as they fixed on her.

"I should have realized that," he said gently. "You do care for me, don't you, Maggie?"

She held back from him. "This is no time to talk of romance. Not on the same day the tragedy of Mabel's death has shattered us all."

Giles looked penitent. "I'm sorry. I'm too impulsive." He allowed her to go free. "This has been a dreadful day."

"And what about that woman with the sick child at home?"

"That one," he said awkwardly. "Oh, I gave her some medicine. Not that I think the child will live. When they go that far, they seldom survive."

"She spoke weirdly of its aging in a few hours."

He sneered. "There was a good deal of imagination in that. You mustn't accept all their wild stories as gospel."

"No," she said. "I suppose not. And yet everyone here wants to believe the unfair rumors that have been spread about Barnabas."

"You're still willing to defend a murderer and a vampire?"

"I don't think such creatures as vampires exist," she said. "And I won't accept Barnabas as a murderer until a court has proved him one."

"That shouldn't take too long," Giles said grimly.

"We'll see."

"The constable will be back this evening to see Barnabas," Giles said. "It should be decided then."

"I wouldn't be surprised," she said, starting up the broad stairway.

He came to the bottom of it. "I'll see you at dinner. Afterward we can talk."

She glanced down at him. "I told you I wasn't feeling well. Dr. West advised me to rest in my room for the night. You can ask the housekeeper to have toast and tea sent up to me."

"But when will we talk?"

"Later." Tinning, she quickly made her way up the stairs. So far things had worked out well. She'd not have to face the others at the dinner table and she'd nicely alibied her visit to town.

When Constable Withers returned his news would be bound to displease most of those at Collinwood. Barnabas would have his freedom assured. But she was beginning to feel Letty was right: Barnabas should leave Collinsport soon before he became involved in worse trouble.

The fog shrouded the grounds. She sat down near the window to watch for the constable's carriage. She was seated there when an easy knock came on her door. When she opened it, Aunt Polly was standing there with a covered tray.

"The housekeeper said you were ill," the stout woman told her. "So I brought you up the tea and toast myself."

"Thank you," Maggie said taking the tray from the old woman's shaky hands. "It was too much for you. You shouldn't have bothered."

"I am the senior female member of the Collins family residing here," Aunt Polly said with dignity. "I have my duty toward our guests."

"Of course," she said. "And you are a truly gracious hostess."

"I was one day, but that was long ago. Too long ago." She moved to the door. "They won't listen to me now. They disturb the spirits and they scoff at the Norris curse. But they'll find out I was right." Still murmuring to herself, the old woman vanished into the shadowed hallway.

Maggie put down the tray and closed the door. Aunt Polly puzzled her. Lately her habitual tartness had given away to a kind of melancholy. And what did her continued references to the Norris curse mean? And then it struck her. Undoubtedly Aunt Polly had resented the influence of one Norris sister and then the other in Collinwood. She had probably endured taking second place to Olive and when Giles' wife had died had assumed she would then be mistress of the household. Instead, Valeria had come to visit and usurped her position again. That would be why she accused Valeria of all kinds of evil plotting and hated her so. Maggie was forced to smile to herself at this simple explanation of the mystery.

CHAPTER 10

The constable's carriage finally arrived at seven. By that time it was almost as dark as late evening, the heavy fog not having lessened at all. Maggie wondered if any news would be brought up to her and decided that this was not likely. She waited. A few minutes after eight she saw the constable walk away from the house and get into his carriage. And before he left he lighted the lantern that hung from it.

Maggie began to feel isolated and uneasy. When would she hear from Barnabas? Asa Collins had announced he would not have his cousin in the house. So she would have to meet him outside. But where and when?

She thought of slipping down the rear stairs and leaving the house by the back door. The chances were that she could manage this without being discovered. Then she could quickly make her way to the old house. There would be someone there to tell her where Barnabas was. He might even be waiting for her himself.

She lighted a candle rather than the lamp. It gave the room enough illumination for the moment. Then she went to the closet to get her cloak. She had just swung it over her shoulders and turned when she glanced across the heavily shadowed room to see the door from the hall move stealthily. Too terrified to stir or speak, she watched the door with fascinated horror.

At last a figure showed in the dark room and she saw that

it was Barnabas. She gave a tiny gasp of relief and ran forward to his arms. He held her close and kissed her. Then he let her go and carefully closed the door.

Turning to her again he spoke in a low voice, "I had to come and thank you for what you did."

She studied his gaunt face by the faint light of the candle on the dresser.

She could barely see his expression. "How did you manage to get up here? Asa said he wouldn't allow you in the house."

Barnabas smiled grimly. "I'm not an invited guest. But I know secret ways of entering Collinwood. In fact, I'd say I know this old house much better than Asa or any of the others."

"Then you have been here before!"

"That's not important," he told her. "The thing that counts is that I'm here with you now. I've been very worried about you."

She smiled wanly. "It has been a busy day. Did the constable give you a clean bill of health?"

"Grudgingly," Barnabas said. "With a warning that I'd better watch myself in the future. And he wouldn't have been all that generous except for you and the owner of the Blue Whale. When he heard what went on in the tavern last night he had to look elsewhere for the murderer."

"Poor Mabel!"

"Yes." The handsome face became grim. "I feared something like this might happen. I would like to avenge her before I leave."

"Then you know who killed her?"

He nodded. "Yes."

She looked up at him anxiously. "You should inform Constable Withers."

"He wouldn't listen to me."

"I suppose not."

"So, as has happened so often before, I must either be patient and allow the culprits to bring about their own punishment or mete out justice myself."

"I've lost all perspective. I'm completely confused. Can you tell me who is to blame?"

He shook his head gravely. "Not yet. It would only place you in more danger. And I don't want to do that." He moved over by the nearest window and gazed out broodingly into the foggy darkness.

"So you're going to take justice in your own hands?"

"It may come to that," he agreed, still staring out at the gloomy night. "But I will wait a little longer. Something is developing here that will change matters greatly."

"Aunt Polly was up here a little while ago. She was filled with chatter of spirits and talked of the Norris curse."

Barnabas turned to her with a questioning look. "What did she say about a curse?"

"Nothing I could understand," Maggie complained. "I guess she's angry at Valeria for taking charge of the household."

"Probably. I'll be going in a few minutes. And while you're alone here, I want you to be especially careful."

She shrugged. "There's little I can do. It's not easy to protect one's self from ghosts."

He frowned. "Have you seen your phantom in pink again?"

"Once since we last met," she told him. "I was in bed. She came out of the shadows and attacked me. I fainted. When I came to your Mrs. Judd was bending over me."

Barnabas' face shadowed for a brief moment. Then in a matter-of-fact voice, he said, "I must question Mrs. Judd about that."

Maggie studied his expression closely. "People claim she is a witch. And she does come in and out of here as easily as you without anyone being the wiser. You don't think she's the one who has made the attacks on me?"

"Do you think she is?"

He had put the question to her very quickly. She hesitated, then said, "No, I guess not."

"You're bound to come to many wild conclusions," he told her in his sympathetic way. "Right now you're undergoing a time of crisis. But it will pass."

She touched a hand to her temple. "It's not being able to remember that makes it all worse. I'm sure if I could think back I'd be able to read the minds of the others better. Understand their motives."

"At least you're seeing them more clearly than you did."

"Why does Asa hate you so?"

Barnabas sighed. "Relations have always been strained between our branches of the family. It began when the first Barnabas Collins decided to live in England."

She nodded thoughtfully. "He claims your ancestor left under some kind of cloud."

"It was long ago. A sad tale. It can't have any bearing on things now," Barnabas said in a manner that indicated he was reluctant to pursue the subject.

"Letty believes you should leave here at once," she said. "And I'm ready to agree with that."

"Not yet."

"There might be another murder and this time you could have more trouble proving your innocence."

"I'll have to chance that."

She looked into the handsome face with worry in her eyes.

"You know they have whispered behind your back that you are a vampire. However mad the accusation is, you have to live it down. And the manner of Mabel's murder was so weird. I mean her body being drained of blood. It suggests a vampire might to be blame, doesn't it?"

"It could suggest many other things," he pointed out. "She could have been the victim of a negligent surgeon."

Maggie's eyes went wide. "Someone like Giles."

"There are many possibilities."

But now she was convinced that he meant Giles had murdered the girl. And she could see that he might have deliberately drained the body of blood so Barnabas would be blamed.

She said, "I didn't tell you that I called on Dr. West when I was in Collinsport today."

Barnabas looked surprised. "No. You didn't."

"I saw him and told him I had serious misgivings about the clinic Giles is operating."

"And what did he say?"

"He suspects what is happening as well. He has seen some children suffering from what appears to be premature aging and he thinks it could be the vaccine Giles is treating them all with."

"If he knows all that, why hasn't he done something about it?"

"Because of the family," she said. "And he is a very retiring man. But he gave me his promise he would look into the clinic business. He's going to call on Giles."

Barnabas smiled grimly. "I'd expect that will give my dear cousin some uneasy moments."

"If only he'll be alarmed enough to stop those dreadful experiments," she said.

"Don't count on it," Barnabas told her. "It will take more than that. But I'm glad you've brought it to Dr. West's attention. Now I must really leave before someone comes up here and discovers me."

"When will I see you again?"

He touched a comforting hand to her arm. "Just as soon as I can arrange it."

"Barnabas, please take care!"

"I'll be all right," he promised. "You are the one that concerns me. Be especially cautious." And he touched his cold lips to her forehead again.

In a moment he was gone. She stood there alone in the candlelit room and wondered whether the meeting between them had been real or if she'd only dreamed it. Remembrance of his embrace and the touch of his icy lips were enough to offer solid proof it had happened.

Those cold lips always troubled her. And his hands were also cool to touch. He was a strange person but surely a charming one. And she could not believe any evil about him. Especially the wild lies Giles offered. Slowly she removed her cloak and hung it up. Now there was scarcely any reason for her to leave the room. Barnabas had warned her to keep to herself, so she decided to go to bed early.

Some time toward morning she was jolted awake by a wailing scream and a distant crash. She sat up in bed to listen but all had become silent again. After staring into the darkness for a few minutes she came to the conclusion the noises had been part of a nightmare. And she went back to sleep once more.

CHAPTER 11

Sunshine returned the next morning. She had just completed dressing when a heavy knock came on her door. When she opened the door, Asa Collins stood grim-faced in the hallway.

"May I come in and speak with you a moment?"

"Of course," she said, stepping back.

He entered with an air of solemn dignity. "I have some sad news for you."

Fear for Barnabas tightened around her heart. "Yes."

"There was a dreadful accident last night."

She recalled the scream that had penetrated her dreams. "I thought I heard a cry," she said. "A wailing cry."

His gray eyes were fixed on her coldly. "Very possibly you did. My sister Polly stumbled and fell the length of the second stairway. She broke her neck and died immediately."

"Oh, no!" she whispered.

Asa nodded. "She was my only sister. The sole member of our generation left. I feel very much alone."

"Of course you would," she agreed sympathetically. "I had come to like her. She often talked with me."

"So I understand," he said in his stem way, studying her.

She felt the power of those icy gray eyes on her. Nervously, she asked, "What was she doing wandering about in the middle of the night? And what could have caused her fall?"

"She hasn't been quite herself lately," Asa said. "It is my belief she became confused and wandered out into the hall. In her dazed state it would be easy for her to trip and fall."

"There was no one around at the time?"

"No. I found her body myself. I hoped she might be alive. I called my son and he pronounced her dead almost the moment he looked at her."

Wild thoughts were racing through her mind. Perhaps Aunt Polly's death had not been a natural one. For some time the old woman had been trying to tell her something. Could she have been waylaid last night on the way to her with a warning? Aunt Polly had hated Valeria and Giles. Maggie believed the two already were murderers; it wouldn't be out of character for them to have caused the old woman's death as well.

"This will make a great change here at Collinwood," she said.

"It will be much different for me," Asa agreed grimly. "Well, now you know."

"Have you made any funeral plans?"

"She will be buried tomorrow in the family cemetery."

"I'd like to be there," she said quietly.

"Thank you," Asa said. And he went on his way.

The news had taken away her appetite. Again she wished that she could go to Barnabas for advice. But she doubted that he was at the old house—and, even if he was, neither Letty nor Mrs. Judd would let her speak to him during his working hours.

The second death at Collinwood had taken place shockingly close after Mabel's murder. Would there be a third? And soon? A cold chill rippled through Maggie's slim body. Was she slated to be the third victim?

Barnabas had said the situation required patience and control. She wondered if she could meet the crisis with his dignified calm. She must at least try. It would mean going downstairs and mingling with the others in the house, pretending she believed it had been an accident. It wasn't going to be easy.

Her breakfast came and she took only a half-piece of toast and a cup of tea. Then, feeling she could postpone it no longer, she went downstairs. Finding the lower level of the house deserted, she stepped out to the warm sunshine of the garden. And there in Aunt Polly's beloved rose garden, in flowing black gown and carrying a parasol of the same shade, was the lovely Valeria Norris. She was moving among the rose bushes snipping off selected buds and placing them in a basket she carried. Maggie at once identified it as Aunt Polly's basket. Hurt welled up in her.

"I see you are busy selecting some of Aunt Polly's choice blooms."

Valeria gave her a supercilious smile. "Yes. I think it fitting to have a bouquet of these roses placed on her casket."

"I see," Maggie said, torn between rage and sorrow, and forced to make no show of the emotions welling within her.

"Do you agree?"

"She loved roses," Maggie replied tightly.

The garden was deathly quiet except for the distant sound of the surf and the snipping of the shears. A bee buzzed by close to them in the lazy heat of the perfect morning.

"Did you just hear about the accident?" Valeria asked casually.

"Yes."

"A wonder something didn't happen to her before," Valeria said, moving on to another rose bush and studying the pink blooms.

"Why did you expect her to have an accident?"

Valeria turned to offer her a mocking glance. "Because she wasn't responsible for her actions or what she said. I warned you about that ages ago."

She swallowed hard. "Yes."

"I'm sure she said all manner of wild things to you. I was embarrassed that you should be bothered by her. At least you won't be plagued by her fantasies any longer."

"No, I won't be," she agreed awkwardly.

She heard the crunch of footsteps in the gravel path and turned to see that Giles was joining them. He wore a look of grim satisfaction. She saw no sign of any grief on the pale countenance.

Halting between them he said, "My father told me I'd find you two out here. The undertaker will be arriving shortly." He turned to Maggie. "I understand father gave you all the details."

She met his glance. "Yes. All that he knew."

Giles looked mildly disconcerted. "What else could there be to know? Aunt Polly wandered in her sleep and fell to her death."

Valeria smiled knowingly. "I think Maggie enjoys inserting drama into everything. And you know how she feels about Collinwood, especially since her accident. I think she would prefer to believe that Aunt Polly came to her death by an evil spirit. Perhaps her phantom in pink attacked the old woman."

She had to clench her fists to keep from responding sharply. "I meant that no one actually saw what happened."

Giles scowled. "Nor was anyone but her liable to be prowling about the house at that hour of the night."

Valeria said, "You mustn't speak ill of Aunt Polly before Maggie. She came to be very fond of the old lady."

"Possibly because she didn't know her well enough," Giles said, "Polly had a tart tongue in her head and seldom failed to use it. Only lately did she show signs of mellowing."

"Your father will miss her," Maggie pointed out.

"My father is her match in disposition," Giles said. "But he should realize now that he can no longer rule the house with an iron hand."

Valeria had almost filled the basket with roses. "I'll take these inside and put them in water. I'm sure I have enough."

"They'll make a nice touch," Giles agreed.

As soon as Valeria had left them Giles came close to Maggie. His eyes held the same unnatural bright look that had alarmed her before. She felt a strong desire to escape, but he was standing deliberately in her path.

"I think I'll go in," she said, making a move to leave.

He stretched out an arm to block her way. "Give me a minute."

She felt nothing but hatred for him, convinced as she was that he and Valeria had stage-managed his aunt's death. And next they were ready to begin on her. "Please. We have nothing to discuss."

"But we have," he insisted. "You know that I love you."

"How can you talk about such things at this time?"

"Aunt Polly was no more than a nuisance to me."

"That is evident," she said with a biting edge. "Still, there is such a thing as respect."

"Let's forget about the old woman," he said with a coldness that shocked her even more. "What about us? Are you going to help me with my experiment?"

"I won't talk about it now!"

The mad eyes were fixed on her. "You don't want to ever discuss it."

She knew she had to evade any more direct replies. "I don't know anything about what you're doing. What you expect of me."

"You don't have to know. Leave that to me."

"We can discuss it after the funeral."

His expression was surly. "That's just an excuse. You don't want to help me."

"What makes you think so?"

"Because I know you're in love with him. That murderer!"

"I'd rather pretend you didn't say that," she told him. "You're being wildly indiscreet."

His eyes narrowed to slits. "What do you mean?"

Her face was flushed. "That you have no right to say such things."

"You are in love with Barnabas."

"That has nothing to do with it!"

"You'd rather give your affection to him, a monster who prowls the darkness to steal the blood of innocents, than turn to me."

"Barnabas is not what you claim him to be!"

Giles' pale face wore a nasty smile. "Before this is over you'll know the truth about him! That he bears the curse of the vampire! I defy him to hide it from you. Ask my father about the first Barnabas!"

But Maggie was no longer listening. She dodged past him and was now hurrying towards the side door of the mansion. Any doubts that he was demented had been settled by the scene between them.

The balance of the day was like a kind of macabre dream. The undertaker arrived and within a short time Aunt Polly's body reposed in state in an elaborate oak casket in a corner of the front parlor. The old woman looked as grim in death as she had in life. Valeria placed the roses on the top of the casket as she'd promised she would. And Asa spent most of his time standing guard in the room.

By evening the word had gotten around and a steady flow of friends from Collinsport began to arrive to pay their respects. Maggie was sickened by the way Valeria and Giles took over and pretended grief for the visitors. She sat quietly in a far corner of the big room.

It was past eight-thirty and great silver candle holders had been set out with white candles. The flickering yellow flames offered an eerie glow in the vast gloomy room. Six or seven neighbors were standing with Asa offering their condolences in low tones. Giles and Valeria stood by themselves in intimate discussion near the foot of the casket. Sitting alone in the distance Maggie felt like an outsider.

All at once a kind of shock seemed to fill the parlor. She saw the others turn toward the doorway and following their lead she glanced that way to see Barnabas standing there very erectly.

He slowly moved into the room and went over beside the casket. He bowed his head a moment to pay homage to Aunt Polly. Maggie saw that Asa was scowling at his cousin but making no move towards him. Valeria and Giles watched the handsome Englishman with obvious uneasiness. The others in the room did not conceal their surprise too well.

The silence continued with all eyes on Barnabas. Then he tinned away from the casket, giving Valeria and Giles a stony glance, and went over to Asa.

Ignoring the old man's indignant glare, he said quietly, "You have my sympathy, Cousin Asa." And then he turned and headed directly across the room towards her. Her heart began to beat wildly. He paused before her and in a low voice said, "Remember what I said. Patience."

"It's very bad."

"I understand." He bowed to her gravely, then turned and walked out. Not until he'd vanished did the murmur of conversation resume in the room once more. Everyone seemed suddenly anxious to pretend that Barnabas had never been there.

Later, when the visitors had left, Asa escorted Maggie up to the door of her room. He paused to say, "Barnabas gave you special attention tonight. Let me warn you his friendship could cost you a great deal."

"I don't understand," she said, staring at the old man's grim face.

"As you are my guest, I have a responsibility toward you. Polly always held such principles important. And so do I. My words are only offered for your good." And with a bow, he said goodnight.

She went into her room in a state of utter depression. Whatever she thought of the others in the house, she was sure that Asa was frank and honest. Did this mean that he knew Barnabas to be evil? She couldn't believe it. And yet the old man rarely made idle statements!

It was too early for bed. She paced up and down the bedroom fitfully, restless and unable to sort out her thoughts.

And then a strange impulse came over her, a desire to go back down to the parlor again and stand by Aunt Polly's casket for a moment. Stand there alone. Something nagged in the back of her mind, telling her this would give her some peace. At last, with some apprehension, she started down the shadowed stairways to view the dead woman.

Silence had fallen over the old mansion. She softly made her way down the stairs and crossed the entrance hall to the parlor. A faint glow of light showed that the candles still burned by the casket. She was just at the point of entering the room when she saw a weird figure standing by the casket. The phantom in pink!

Stifling a scream, Maggie swiftly retreated to the concealment of the opposite doorway and waited. It was not long before the phantom came silently by her like a pink shadow. She watched with horrified fascination as the apparition in pink cowl and flowing dress moved quickly up the stairs.

When she thought it was safe, she followed. She reached the second landing in time to see the phantom figure vanish down the corridor in the area of the bricked off room!

CHAPTER 12

Maggie remained there in the shadows watching for long minutes after the phantom had disappeared. And now she was sure that this was no ghost but a living person in some way in league with Giles. It was likely the apparition had vanished into his room, which adjoined the bricked-up door of his dead wife's bedroom.

But what did it all mean? Why had Giles used the ghostly creature to terrify her? And what was really going on in this grim house of mystery? Aunt Polly had known, but in her addled state had not been able to properly explain. And Aunt Polly had died for her knowledge!

With bated breath she continued to crouch there. And then she saw another figure making its way up the corridor. This time it was Giles. He came as far as the stairs, looking neither to the right or the left, and then started down. When a safe amount of time had elapsed, she decided, she would try to discover just where the phantom had gone.

She knew she was taking a chance but she felt reasonably sure Giles would remain downstairs for a while. Soundlessly she neared his door; it was a trifle ajar. She halted and waited tensely. Then she very slowly opened it a bit more so she could see all of his room. It was decorated and furnished well, somewhat like her own. Gathering courage, she took a few steps inside.

The door leading to the adjoining room was open – the room whose hall door had been bricked up by the supposedly grieving Giles.

And it was in use. She nervously approached the door, finally stepping inside the room that Olive Collins had once had as her own. And she received a second shock! The entire bedroom was decorated in a shade of pink that exactly matched the robes of the phantom. She stood in the center of the eerie room. Pink walls, pink drapes, the carpet in the same shade and even the bed coverings matching. It was the kind of a single-tone room you might conceive in a nightmare. It had no bearing on reality. It was a place of madness!

This was her last thought before she was seized in an iron grip and a hand was clamped over her mouth. She tried to scream and struggled wildly but the person who had come up silently behind her was no weak opponent. As she fought to free herself her terrified eyes caught a glimpse of a smiling Valeria, who had come into the room and closed the door.

Valeria came near her and advised, "You'd do well to save your strength. None of this will help you."

Maggie's reply was to renew her struggles and then her arm was wrenched with such a torturing pain that she blacked out.

When she came to, she was stretched out on her back with a sneering Giles staring down at her. She tried to raise herself and found she couldn't. She was strapped down. It was then she remembered the table in the laboratory with the hanging straps and with her eyes widening with horror she took in the shadowed surroundings. She was a prisoner in the laboratory and strapped to that sinister operating table.

"No!" she cried out.

"Sorry I had to handle you so roughly," he said. "But you refused to behave."

"Let me free!" she demanded, struggling vainly against the stout leather straps.

"That will do you no good."

"Why have you brought me here?"

Giles studied her, the mad light in his eyes more apparent than ever before. "You delivered yourself to us," he said softly. "It was lovely. We set the stage and you did exactly what we wanted. Did you think those doors were left open by accident? Or that I didn't expect you to go all the way into the pink room?"

"I'll be missed. Your father won't let you harm me!"

Giles chuckled. "But he won't blame me. He'll be positive Barnabas is the guilty one. Who else would want your blood but Barnabas?"

Maggie stared up at him aghast. "My blood?"

"I'm getting ahead of my story," he told her. "When my wife suffered her dreadful illness she became mad. Knowing she had deteriorated into a haggard witch, she came to believe that when she wore pink it concealed her ugliness. So I catered to her whims and bought her clothes of pink. I even had that room up there decorated in delicate pink to satisfy her. Wouldn't you call that being a thoughtful husband?"

"You're insane!"

"Insanity is a common trait," Giles told her quite cheerfully. "All the world is mad in one way or another. But we are safe as long as our madness is properly restrained. I think I have carefully concealed mine."

"Dr. West knows better. I told him about you and the sham of your experiments. Of the poison you've been feeding those poor consumptives."

"The poor consumptives you refer to so touchingly have been assisting me in a noble purpose," Giles said grandly. "True, they have not realized their share in the experiments. But when my name is famous they will have made their contribution. And no one will question the methods I used to gain my objective. Successful men are rarely bothered in such matters."

"Let me go," Maggie pleaded. "I'll explain you're mentally ill and do what I can to help you!"

His smile was not pleasant to see. "I don't need your help. It is you who happen to be the prisoner. Thanks to the secret passages of Collinwood I had no trouble bringing you down here from the room above."

She was fast losing hope. But she wasn't going to give him the satisfaction of knowing it. "Barnabas will settle with you," she warned him. "If you harm me in any way Barnabas will avenge me."

His expression became grim. "Barnabas will have a stake through his heart. They'll come upon him in the secret room in the old house where he sleeps by day and drag him from his coffin and pierce his heart with a stake of hemlock." Giles crouched close over her so that she could feel his warm breath. The mad eyes became all-consuming. "And Barnabas will disintegrate and crumble to dust and corruption as he should have a century ago!"

"You're mad!" she sobbed, exerting all her strength against the straps and not freeing herself to the slightest extent.

"That will be the end of Barnabas the vampire. And he'll die that way because he'll be the one accused of murdering you."

"And you are the killer," she cried. "You murdered poor Mabel."

"Mabel was a subject in the final step of my experiment," Giles said straightening up. "The final step before I claim success through you. You should be pleased to know that your death will mark a milestone in the progress of medicine. That is what eminent surgeons sometimes tell their patients. Some must die so others may live. I'm merely following in a great tradition."

As he finished speaking the drapes at the other end of the room parted and Valeria appeared, still clad in the revealing lace dressing gown she had worn upstairs. She went straight to Giles without glancing down at Maggie. "What do you plan to do?" she asked urgently.

The two appeared demonic in this dimly-lighted room filled with test tubes, medical paraphernalia and other apparatus. They both were plainly on edge.

Giles said, "We'll go ahead. No point in delaying now."

Valeria's lovely face registered fear. "I'm frightened."

"We've planned and waited for this moment," the young doctor said, taking her roughly by the arms. "I haven't gone through all this to wind up with you becoming hysterical and failing me."

"I'm not ready," she pleaded.

"You'll never be more ready," he told her. "And if you don't go through with it, you know the price you'll have to pay!"

"I have time!" she protested.

"Little time. Weeks perhaps, or months at the most. We have to work fast now that we have the girl here." Valeria closed her eyes for a brief second as if to fight for control. Then she raised her head and looked at him with dull resignation. "All right. I'm willing."

"Good," he said, still holding onto her arms. "What about upstairs?"

"I turned the lock," Valeria said. "We won't be disturbed."

"Then there's nothing to hold us back," Giles said with a sigh of relief. "You'll take the sofa. I'll bring it close to the operating table. Unless there's some hitch we should have the whole thing finished in an hour." He moved to the other side of the room to drag the sofa over.

Valeria looked down at her. "So now you know why we brought you here from Boston."

She stared up at her in disbelief. "Surely you'll help me. Make him realize he's making a mad mistake."

"No mistake," Valeria said with a grave look on her lovely face. "We invited you here for this. We didn't plan your accident. That held us up for a while."

They meant to kill her! The intent was clearly there in Valeria's dull tone as she spoke of their plans. And Maggie still didn't know the reason she must be sacrificed.

Undoubtedly Valeria had enacted the role of the phantom in pink and led her to be taken prisoner. She and Giles had been partners in crime, just as Aunt Polly had insisted. Could file Norris curse be the curse of madness?

She found herself speaking her thoughts aloud. "The Norris curse," she repeated in a weak voice.

Valeria looked alarmed. "What do you know about the Norris curse?" And she turned to Giles who was dragging up the sofa. "She knows!"

He straightened up from his exertions, smiling grimly. "I don't think she knows. But it's high time we told her."

"She does know! She said so just now! She mentioned the Norris curse!"

Giles furrowed his brow. "Why did you mention the Norris curse? Where did you hear of it?"

Maggie didn't have any idea why they both should suddenly be so concerned. But it gave her a small sense of power to realize how much her words had bothered them. "Aunt Polly told me!"

He smiled derisively. "She didn't tell you much because she didn't know much. But I'll be glad to offer you a full explanation."

Valeria was clutching at his arm. "Giles! We haven't time!"

He brushed her off impatiently. "We have all the night. And she does have a right to know."

"I have a feeling about it," Valeria protested. "It's my secret."

"She should know," he insisted. "It is her blood that will save you."

"Giles!" Valeria sobbed in protest and sank down on the sofa with her head bowed.

Maggie still had no idea why her reference to the curse should cause such consternation. But she was well aware of one thing. She had gained some time and brought about an argument between the two. If she could engage Giles in conversation long enough anything might happen. Barnabas might even discover her missing from her room and come to her rescue. It was a slim hope but the only one she had.

Looking up into Giles' eyes, she said, "Tell me."

He nodded. "I learned about the Norris curse a few months after I married Olive. She had kept it from me until then. It was a disease that had attacked the female members of her family all down through the years. It didn't strike until the Norris women were at their loveliest in their mid-twenties. And then it struck them down mercilessly."

"You mean it killed them?"

"Worse than that," Giles said, the terror of it showing on his face. "It was a process of accelerated aging. Within the period of a few months these lovely creatures aged years. And within two or three years they died of old age. Died looking like ninety or a hundred-year-olds. Can you picture what that would be like for a lovely woman and the man married to her?"

Even in her desperate straits Maggie was horrified at the story. "And that is what happened to Olive?"

"Yes," he said. "And what will happen to Valeria in weeks or months unless I save her. And through you I will save her."

"I don't understand yet."

"You condemned me for working to perfect my vaccine," Giles continued. "And for taking advantage of the patients visiting my consumptive's clinic. Of course I used them as test animals. And many of them died. But they were going to die soon anyway."

Filled with revulsion, she nonetheless forced herself to hear him out. It was her only means of gaining precious minutes. And fortunately Valeria was proving no problem. She still sat with bowed head on the sofa.

Maggie argued, "You had no right."

"I had the right of genius," Giles contradicted her. "I found a vaccine that produced the accelerating process and aged children years in the passing of a day. And I learned the only way the disease could be halted was to completely exchange the blood of the victim with that of a healthy person."

"And that is what happened to Mabel's blood?"

"Her blood saved a child's life."

"A child you had condemned to death by infecting it with the disease in the first place."

"Mabel was a tribute to science," he told her. "And now you will save Valeria's life and beauty with your blood."

"You're mad!" she cried. "It won't work! It can't work!"

"It has to work," Giles told her sternly. "Valeria is the great love of my life. I never cared for Olive as I do for her. And now she can be saved, before the disease strikes. Once it has started its inroads there is no halting it. It is too late! She must have your blood now while she's still in health."

Maggie turned her head. "Valeria, don't listen to him! He'll kill us both!"

Valeria was on her feet now, her expression resigned. "I have complete faith in Giles. There is no other hope for me."

Giles patted her arm. "I knew you'd find your courage," he said. "We'll start at once. You can help me assemble the things."

Maggie felt the panic rising in her. On the verge of hysteria, she cried, "Wait! Please! If the blood transfer really works, why didn't you try it on Olive?" It was a frantic effort to delay what seemed the inevitable for seconds longer.

Before he could reply, a querulous female voice, the voice of an ancient, came from the end of the room. "Yes, Giles, why didn't you try it on Olive?"

Maggie saw the phantom in pink standing before the drapes. It was the same withered face, the same expression of hatred, but now the ghost was holding a pistol in her hand. And the weapon was directed at Giles.

Giles registered shock. "You!"

"Me," the wavering voice replied sarcastically. "I may be a doddering old wreck but I'm still smarter than my sister. She thought she'd locked me up safely. But I had a second key. And I'm here to ask why she is being given the operation instead of me?"

Valeria was huddled close to Giles, staring at the ancient crone in terror. "Because you can't be saved now! Once the disease strikes it's too late! You'll be dying of old age in a few weeks. It doesn't matter!"

"That's true," Giles joined in plaintively. "I'd have saved you if I could. I've kept you hidden here. Pretended you were dead. Saved your pride."

The old woman shook her head. "No, Giles, you used me! You used me in your efforts to save her. She was the one you always loved! So you let this happen to me!" The voice had risen to a high-pitched sob and as Olive Collins finished she fired at Giles. With a cry and a surprised look he clutched his abdomen and collapsed on the floor.

Valeria stumbled back, her lovely face distorted by fear. She held up her hands plaintively. "Please!"

The hag's withered face showed only scorn as she fired the pistol again and Valeria slumped down on the floor beside Giles with a sigh. Now the phantom walked slowly toward the operating table, the pistol pointed at Maggie. "Now you," she said, her finger on the trigger.

Maggie closed her eyes. No use to plead. No hope left. "It won't do, Olive!" Barnabas' voice rang out with authority from the area of the drapes. Maggie opened her eyes in time to see him standing there.

The phantom in pink whirled around swiftly and fired twice at Barnabas. But the bullets appeared not to have hit him. He came slowly forward to her. The pistol dropped from her hands and with a scream she turned and fled out the door leading to the cellar.

Barnabas came to Maggie and began unbuckling the straps holding her. "Let her go," he murmured. "She's settled all our debts for us, just as I said would happen." He helped Maggie sit up and rubbed her wrists and ankles to help restore the circulation. "Feeling better?"

She nodded weakly and leaned against him for a moment. Then she whispered, "What about them?"

"I'll see," he said. And he left her to examine them. In a few minutes he was at her side again. "Valeria died right away. Giles breathed his last as I bent over him. I'll get you upstairs."

"I don't know whether I can walk or not."

"I'll carry you," he said. "You can't remain here in this charnel house." And he swung her up into his arms easily. "I'll take you up by the secret passage."

She clung to him. "I was so afraid. But the bullets didn't hit you."

He gave her a sad, thoughtful look. "No, they didn't harm me."

She was too upset at the time to notice the subtle change he'd made in her statement. But later she did remember. And she also realized that Olive could hardly have missed him at such short range, after gunning down the other two with such deadly accuracy. But days would pass before Maggie would go over all this in her mind.

Barnabas took her to her own room and placed her gently on

her bed, then stood above her in darkness broken only by the glow of a single candle. In some strange way she knew that this was probably her last chance to tell him what was in her heart.

Still weak from her ordeal she stared up at him. "Thank you, Barnabas. You know that I love you."

He nodded. "I know." And he took one of her hands in his. "Remember me. I'm going now. Let the old man find the others in the laboratory."

She found the strength to sit up and clutch his hand. "Barnabas, I'm afraid. Don't leave me."

"I have no choice now," he told her sadly. "But perhaps in another happier day we'll meet again."

"You're in love with Letty," she reproved him.

His handsome face wore a gentle smile. "You always phrase things wrongly. Letty is in love with me. And that is good and right for this year of 1880. We must look to the future for any happiness that might be ours."

He bent and kissed her. It was a lasting kiss and when it ended he left her. She sank back on the pillow, her eyes brimming with tears and then everything became a blank. She awoke to the gray of morning. And it was shortly after that that Asa came to her room with word of the tragedy in the laboratory.

The double shooting following on the accidental death of Aunt Polly and murder of the maid created a sensation in the village. When Olive's withered and battered body was found on the rocks below Widows' Hill it was easy for Asa and the townspeople to reconstruct the tragedy.

As Asa Collins put the story together, Olive, who had been insane, was responsible for all that had happened. He blamed her for shoving Aunt Polly down the stairs to her death. And he condemned Giles for pretending that his mad wife was dead when she was actually alive and hidden in the old mansion. Valeria also had been in on the secret and in the end had paid for it with her life when Olive had turned on both of them. The weird drama had ended with Olive a suicide from the cliff.

Maggie heard the story and knew how wrong it was, but she let the story stand. Better to avoid any scandal that could be avoided, and in any case she doubted that the townspeople would believe the true story. Of course Mabel's murder was still left unexplained, but the general feeling remained that Barnabas was the killer, even though Constable Withers pointed out there was no proof to back up such suspicions.

In any event Barnabas and two women had vanished on the night of the murders at Collinwood. The following morning, as soon as Maggie felt well enough, she hurried to the old house and was startled to see that its front door was open. She went inside and discovered it was empty. They were all gone. It wasn't unexpected; Barnabas had warned her. Still, she felt a deep sorrow as she walked back to Collinwood.

The tragedy mellowed Asa a good deal. He was a lonely old man and he begged Maggie to remain with him for a few weeks until he'd made some adjustment to all that had taken place. She forced herself to do it for several reasons. One was that her memory had still not returned. And the others were her sympathy for the old man and her hope that Barnabas might come back to see her again, even if only briefly.

Asa Collins was keen enough to sense her great affection for the handsome Englishman, and gradually he left off making bitter comments about him. When he mentioned him at all he would speak with a quiet respect.

Yet it came as a surprise to her when she returned from a long walk by the cliffs one late afternoon to find him in the entrance hall directing one of the servants in the hanging of a portrait on the wall. It was the portrait of the original Barnabas Collins, the one he'd ordered removed from the living room many weeks back.

He turned to her with one of his gruff looks. "I think he might fit well there, don't you?"

"Yes," she said, pleased at his action. "It takes the bare look from the hallway."

Asa studied the newly hung portrait. "It is a strong face. In a way I have missed him."

And that was that. She knew enough about the old man's ways not to make any long conversation about it. He had come around to her way of thinking enough to tolerate the portrait again. It was a victory; she need not press it.

That evening after dinner as a gesture to please him, she said, "I'm going to take some roses to Aunt Polly's grave. They'll die if I don't. And I feel she'd like them."

Asa nodded. "Polly was mighty fond of that rose garden."

She didn't ask him to go with her but left him contentedly puffing his pipe on the side veranda. At least a measure of peace had been restored to Collinwood. The horror of the sham clinic was only a vague memory. And Asa had arranged with Dr. West to have a proper clinic for victims of consumption built near the village. It would be a place where they would receive the best treatment. So out of great evil had come good.

Maggie sighed as she recalled Barnabas asking for patience. She felt little of it these days. Passing the old house, which had been closed up since Barnabas' departure, she wondered if she would ever see him again. And again that nagging started at the back of her head, that voice which insisted the life she was living at this moment was all a dream, that her real existence was somewhere else, in another time. It was frightening.

She walked down the hill to the cemetery and the fresh graves. She stopped by Aunt Polly's grave and placed the roses on it. Aunt Polly had tried to warn her and she felt deep affection for the memory of the stout woman.

After a little she came to the graves of Giles and Olive Collins. Asa had insisted they be buried side by side. Some distance away was the grave of Valeria Norris, who the old man considered had turned the affair into a tragedy. He blamed her for turning the head of Giles and causing all the trouble. In a way he didn't understand, he was right.

"I'll be building a fine tomb for Giles and Olive one day," he had told Maggie, "but Valeria will not share it." Staring at the graves, she wondered what would really happen. Suddenly she sensed someone was standing beside her. She turned to see who it was. And it was Barnabas! He looked as handsome as ever in his caped coat and his smile had all his familiar charm.

"Barnabas!" she exclaimed. "I knew you'd come!"

"I never break a promise," he told her. And his eyes met hers.

"It's dusk," she gasped. "You always come at dusk!" She meant to say a lot of other things. But a great roaring was filling her ears and her head was in a whirl. Her vision blurred and she reached out for him as the shadows closed in around her.

She opened her eyes. "Where am I?"

Barnabas was cradling her head and shoulders in his arms as she lay on the ground. "Outside the Giles Collins tomb in the old cemetery," he told her. "I took you inside to show you the coffin of Valeria Norris in the secret room old Asa Collins had built for it and you fainted on me."

"I'm sorry. That was stupid of me."

Barnabas laughed lightly. "My fault," he said. "It was damp and unpleasant in there. We'd better get back to Collinwood or Elizabeth will be calling me down."

She sighed. "I suppose so." And she let him help her to her feet. "It's almost dark."

He nodded. "We'll see some stars before we get back." They started out of the cemetery and up the hill. Suddenly, she said, "The Norris curse!"

And she halted. Barnabas glanced at her. "The what?"

"The Norris curse," she said. "It seems to be a phrase ringing in my mind. It must have come to me when I fainted."

Barnabas smiled wisely. "Yes, it must have." And they walked on.

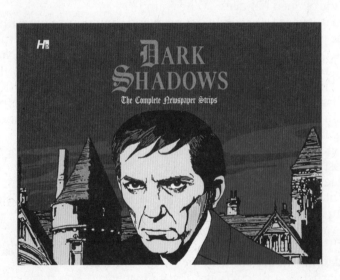